ANIMAL WATCH

A Visual Introduction to
MONKEYS
AND APES

ANIMAL WATCH

A Visual Introduction to

MONKEYS

AND APES

A Cherrytree Book

Created by Firecrest Books Ltd
Copyright © 2002 Evans Brothers Ltd
First paperback edition published 2002

First UK edition published 2000
by Cherrytree Press
327 High Street
Slough, Berkshire SL1 1TX

A subsidiary of Evans Brothers Limited

British Library Cataloguing in Publication Data

Stonehouse, Bernard
Monkeys and apes. – (Animal watch)
1.Monkeys – Juvenile literature 2.Apes – Juvenile literature
3.Monkeys – Behaviour – Juvenile literature
4.Apes – Behaviour – Juvenile literature
I.Title
599.8

ISBN 1 84234 116 2

Printed and bound in Spain

ANIMAL WATCH

A *Visual Introduction to*

MONKEYS

AND APES

Bernard Stonehouse

CHERRYTREE BOOKS

PICTURE CREDITS

Pages 8-9: Oxford Scientific Films

Pages 10-11: Still Pictures

Pages 12-13: Planet Earth; Woodfall Wild Images; Still Pictures

Pages 14-15: BBC Natural History Unit Picture Library; Planet Earth

Pages 16-17: Natural History Photographic Agency;
Oxford Scientific Films

Pages 18-19: BBC Natural History Unit Picture Library;
Oxford Scientific Films; Frank Lane Picture Agency

Pages 20-21: Natural History Photographic Agency; Still Pictures

Pages 22-23: Planet Earth; BBC Natural History Unit Picture Library

Pages 24-25: Planet Earth; Frank Lane Picture Agency;
Natural History Photographic Agency

Pages 26-27: Woodfall Wild Images; BBC Natural History Unit
Picture Library

Pages 28-29: BBC Natural History Unit Picture Library

Pages 30-31: BBC Natural History Unit Picture Library; Still Pictures;
Natural History Photographic Agency

Pages 32-33: BBC Natural History Unit Picture Library; Planet Earth

Pages 34-35: Still Pictures; BBC Natural History Unit Picture Library

Pages 36-37: Frank Lane Picture Agency

Pages 38-39: Still Pictures; Oxford Scientific Films;
Frank Lane Picture Agency

Pages 40-41: Natural History Photographic Agency;
Topham Picturepoint

Pages 42-43: Woodfall Wild Images; Oxford Scientific Films

All satellite mapping: WorldSat

Artwork by

Richard Orr/Bernard Thornton Artists Cover, pp14-25, 28-29

Martin Camm pp8-9, 12-13, 32-33, 36-39

Lucia Guarnotta pp10-11, 30-31, 42-43

Gabriele Maschietti pp24 (talapoin), 26-27

Art and editorial direction by **Peter Sackett**

Edited by **Norman Barrett**

Designed by **Paul Richards, Designers & Partners**

Picture research by **Lis Sackett**

Colour separation by **BrightArts, Singapore**

CONTENTS

INTRODUCING THE PRIMATES

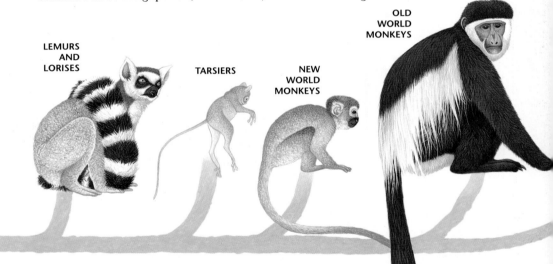

The animals closest to humans.

PRIMATES

Monkeys, apes and humans are all included in a group of mammals called the Primates. Mammals are warm-blooded animals that feed their young on milk. Biologists divide them into about 20 different groups, called orders. Other orders of mammals include Cetacea (whales and dolphins), Carnivora (cats, dogs and other meateaters), Rodentia (rats, mice, squirrels), Pinnipedia (seals and walruses), Insectivora (hedgehogs and shrews) and Chiroptera (bats).

Carolus Linnaeus, a Swedish biologist who lived in the 1700s, was the first to classify animals into natural groups. He regarded humans as the highest of all creatures, so he put them into the order called 'Primates', meaning 'first'. When he saw that monkeys and apes were in many ways similar to humans, he classified them as primates, too. Then three other groups of mammals, the lemurs, lorises and tarsiers, were found to be similar to monkeys, and included as well.

RELATIONSHIPS

In grouping animals together, Linnaeus was not suggesting that they were closely related. He implied only that they were similar in ways that seemed important. Ideas that animals within groups are closely related, and must have 'evolved' from common ancestors, came later (see page 41).

Monkeys and apes are our closest relatives in the animal kingdom. Together with humans and three other groups of mammals, they make up the order of Primates. The 'family tree' below shows how the different groups of Primates may be related to each other.

On the left are some representatives of the Prosimii (see panel below). This suborder contains over 30 living species (different kinds) of animals, mostly cat-sized or smaller. Lemurs live only on the big island of Madagascar and a few smaller islands off the east coast of Africa. Lorises and bush babies live in Africa and southern Asia. In the middle are the Tarsoidea, a much smaller group of only three or four living species. About as big as rats or young rabbits, these too live in trees, in some of the island forests of southeastern Asia.

On the right is a selection of the

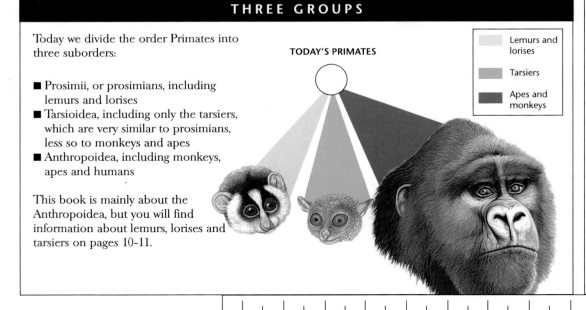

LEMURS AND LORISES

TARSIERS

NEW WORLD MONKEYS

OLD WORLD MONKEYS

THREE GROUPS

Today we divide the order Primates into three suborders:

- Prosimii, or prosimians, including lemurs and lorises
- Tarsioidea, including only the tarsiers, which are very similar to prosimians, less so to monkeys and apes
- Anthropoidea, including monkeys, apes and humans

This book is mainly about the Anthropoidea, but you will find information about lemurs, lorises and tarsiers on pages 10-11.

TODAY'S PRIMATES

Lemurs and lorises

Tarsiers

Apes and monkeys

WHAT MAKES A PRIMATE?

Though lorises, monkeys, apes and humans are at first sight very different, they have several important features in common − important enough for them all to be grouped together as Primates:

- They walk on flat feet, not on their toes like cats and dogs, and their feet have padded soles

- The thumbs (often the big toes, too) are usually separate, so that they can grasp and hold branches and other objects

- Their toes and fingers mostly have flat nails, not claws

Anthropoidea, the main suborder of Primates. This is a much bigger group, containing about 130 species of monkeys, 10 species of apes, and just one species of humans. Most of the monkeys are small, living in trees in or near forests, mainly in tropical and temperate regions. Apes tend to be larger. They live in trees, too, and also on the ground, in warm forested country. About 5 million years ago, some of the apes living in Africa began to change. They left the forests and began to live in more open country. They walked with a more upright posture and their brains became larger. Biologists believe that these apes gradually evolved into the first humans.

APES

Note: The weights and other measurements given in this book, unless otherwise indicated, are for an average adult male

- The two bones that make up the lower arm and leg are separate, so the hands and feet can twist and turn

- They have a large brain, and a large, rounded skull to contain it

- The eyes look forward rather than sideways

- The milk glands are on the chest, not on the abdomen

- They grow slowly, staying longer in the care of their parents than most other mammals

Where they live

WHERE MONKEYS AND APES COME FROM

Millions of years ago the world's continents existed as one great landmass, across which animals could roam freely. By 100 million years ago this landmass had started to split into the continents we know today, each developing its own populations of reptiles, birds and mammals.

Australia broke away from the other continents before most of the mammalian orders appeared. Bats were able to fly there, but the only other native Australian land mammals are the marsupials and the egg-laying monotremes. The primates and other later-evolving mammals could not reach Australia.

When Madagascar parted from Africa about 50 million years ago, the prosimian primates had come into existence, but not monkeys and apes. Prosimians survived in

Tarsier munching a juicy insect

Madagascar and evolved into a variety of forms unknown anywhere else in the world.

Elsewhere, most of the prosimians died out because they could not compete with the newly evolved monkeys.

As North and South America separated from Europe, Africa and Asia, different kinds of monkeys appeared in the 'New World' and 'Old World' (see page 13), and apes began to inhabit the forests of Africa and Asia.

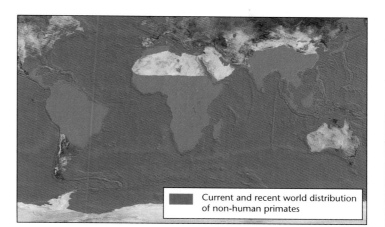

Current and recent world distribution of non-human primates

Primates live in most parts of the world, but different groups within the order live in different localities. Lemurs live only in Madagascar and the nearby Comoro Islands. Lorises and bush babies are found in the forests of Africa, India, Sri Lanka and southeastern Asia. Tarsiers have a more limited range in Indonesia and the Philippine Islands.

Monkeys are widespread in tropical and temperate forests of Central and South America. In Europe they occur only in Gibraltar, but they range widely across Africa and southern Arabia to India, Sri Lanka and southeastern Asia, then north into China and Japan.

Apes are native to Africa and southeastern Asia. The first humans probably appeared in Africa, but now humans are at home all over the world.

THE FIRST PRIMATES

The oldest fossils that we recognize as primates occur in rocks formed about 100 million years ago. Small animals, about the size of rats, they lived in trees and probably fed on insects. Though only their fossil bones and teeth survive, scientists think they must have looked rather like the tree shrews that today live in forests of southeastern Asia. Indeed, some biologists classify modern tree shrews in the order Primates.

Tree shrew – sometimes classified as a primate

LEMURS, LORISES AND TARSIERS

Distant cousins of monkeys and apes.

FACT FILE

RING-TAILED LEMUR

Suborder:	Prosimii
Family:	Lemuridae
Scientific name:	*Lemur catta*
Colour:	Grey body, white face, black nose and eye rings, black and white ringed tail
Weight:	3 kg (6 lb 10 oz)
Length, head and body:	45 cm (18 in)
Habitat:	Forest trees and clearings
Range:	Madagascar

SLENDER LORIS

Suborder:	Prosimii
Family:	Loridae
Scientific name:	*Loris tardigradus*
Colour:	Grey-brown body, white face with black eye rings
Weight:	300 g (11 oz)
Length, head and body:	24 cm (9 in)
Habitat:	Forest trees
Range:	Southern India, Sri Lanka

SPECTRAL TARSIER

Suborder:	Tarsioidea
Family:	Tarsiidae
Scientific name:	*Tarsius spectrum*
Colour:	Grey body, tufted tail
Weight:	110 g (4 oz)
Length, head and body:	12 cm (5 in)
Habitat:	Forest trees
Range:	Sulawesi (Indonesia)

RELATIONSHIPS

Lemurs and lorises make up the suborder Prosimii. The 22 species of lemurs, arranged in four separate families, are generally cat-like but they have long fingers and toes that grasp and wrap around the branches. Lorises and the much more active bush babies are smaller than many of the lemurs and they make up a distinct family of ten species. Tarsiers are even smaller - about the size of rats. The three living species form their own suborder - Tarsioidea.

THESE RING-TAILED LEMURS, sunning themselves in a forest clearing in southwestern Madagascar, live in small troops and move around together by day. Lemurs spend much of their time in the trees, climbing and leaping through the branches. Holding on tightly with fingers and toes, they browse on leaves, shoots and fruit. Sharp noses, pointed ears and prominent round eyes give them an inquiring, alert expression. Nearly all have long furry tails, which they wave in the air as signals to each other.

Lorises are similar but smaller, with rounded ears, large eyes, no tail, and a slightly worried expression. The slender loris of India and Sri Lanka spends its days asleep in a tree, rolled into a ball with head tucked in, and firmly gripping the branches with long fingers and toes. At night it uncurls and patrols slowly

Ring-tailed lemurs

through the branches, catching insects and other small creatures. Pottos, bush babies (galagos) and angwantibos are African relatives of the lorises. They are all nocturnal and feed mainly on insects and fruit.

Tiny tarsiers, with snub-noses and enormous, wondering eyes, have long thin limbs and splayed, padded fingers. They, too, are nocturnal, and almost entirely carnivorous, hunting insects, lizards and birds.

FAMILY LIFE

Ring-tailed lemurs live in groups of a dozen or more adults of both sexes, with perhaps up to a dozen young that move about the forest together. They mate during March and April, and the single young are born about five months later. Within a few minutes of birth the babies are strong enough to hold on to their mothers' fur, and for several weeks they travel piggy-back.

Slender lorises live alone, nocturnal and solitary, keeping out of each other's way except during the breeding seasons. Females mate mainly in November and May, and each gives birth to a single baby five to six months later.

Spectral tarsiers live together in pairs, patrolling territories in the forests, often accompanied by one or two young. Most babies are born in November and December, and they can climb when only a few months old.

Slender loris

Spectral tarsier

Where they live

All of these species live in tropical rainforests. Ring-tailed lemurs live in Madagascar, off the southeastern coast of Africa. Other species of lemurs are found only in Madagascar or on the neighbouring Comoro Islands. The slender loris inhabits the forests of southern India and Sri Lanka. The very similar slow loris, also forest-living, extends from India to Indonesia. Spectral tarsiers live in Sulawesi, east of Borneo, and on forested islands close by. Of the other two species of tarsier, one is found in Borneo and Sumatra, the other in the Philippine Islands. Pottos, bush babies and angwantibos live in forests of tropical Africa.

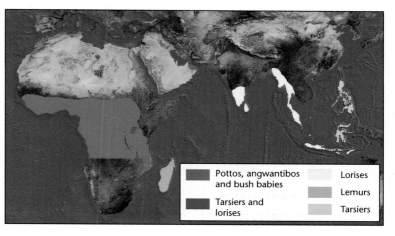

■ Pottos, angwantibos and bush babies	□ Lorises
■ Tarsiers and lorises	■ Lemurs
	■ Tarsiers

SIGHT, HEARING AND SCENT

Like most other primates, prosimians have broad faces with eyes facing forward and slightly outwards. This gives them good forward vision, probably enabling them to judge distances, just as we can. The loris's relatively large eyes, and the huge eyes of tarsiers, help them to see sharply in poor light.

All have relatively large ears, with flaps that can be turned to pick up sounds from different directions. Less obvious is their acute sense of smell. Most of these animals mark their paths along the tree branches with urine, which others of their own kind recognize. Lemurs

Lemurs looking and listening

produce a musky scent from glands on their hands and arms, which probably enables other lemurs to identify them as individuals. By whisking their tails across the glands, they transfer some of the scent to the fur. Waving their tails in the air spreads the scent more widely.

COMBING THE FUR

All mammals have to keep their skin and fur clean, and if possible free from fleas, ticks and other parasites. Most use their claws for scratching, and their tongue for washing and combing. Prosimians have another way – a special comb, made from the front teeth of their lower jaw, which they pull through the fur to keep it in good order. Then they push forward a horny plate under the tongue to keep the comb clean.

Red-bellied lemur

FACT FILE

PATAS MONKEY

Suborder:	Anthropoidea
Family:	Cercopithidae
Scientific name:	*Erythrocebus patas*
Colour:	Reddish-brown back, pale underparts, darker head with black face, white moustache and beard
Weight:	Males 12 kg (26 lb), females 6 kg (13 lb)
Length, head and body:	Males 60 cm (24 in), females 50 cm (20 in)
Habitat:	Grassy plains with trees and shrubs; forest edge
Range:	Senegal, Central Africa, Ethiopia, Kenya, Tanzania

PYGMY CHIMPANZEE (BONOBO)

Suborder:	Anthropoidea
Family:	Pongidae
Scientific name:	*Pan paniscus*
Colour:	Black fur, grey or white skin
Weight:	Males 38 kg (84 lb), female 30 kg (66 lb)
Length, head and body:	75 cm (30 in)
Habitat:	Tropical rainforest
Range:	Congo (Dem Rep)

EARLY HUMAN

Suborder:	Anthropoidea
Family:	Hominidae
Scientific name:	*Homo erectus*
Colour:	Probably brown hair and skin
Weight:	Unknown; probably up to 45 kg (100 lb)
Length, head and body:	Probably up to 1.5 m (5 ft)
Habitat:	Forest edge, grassland
Range:	East Africa, Java, China, possibly worldwide

MONKEY, APES AND HUMANS

The animals most like us – and ourselves.

ONKEYS, APES AND HUMANS are built to very similar plans, with important similarities and differences that reflect their different ways of living.

Monkeys are the smallest, typically about the size of house cats, though some are much smaller and others bigger. They have long limbs, and long fingers and toes. Nearly all live in trees, running and climbing among the branches. A few species, such as baboons, live mainly on the ground, but can still climb well when they need to. Tree-living monkeys tend to have long, well-muscled hind-limbs and relatively short forelimbs. Those that live mainly on the ground have longer arms. Nearly all have tails. The tree-living monkeys have long tails, sometimes longer than the body, which help them to balance. Some South American monkeys have a prehensile (grasping) tail, with a muscular tip that wraps around branches and grasps like an extra hand (see page 17). Ground-living species usually have shorter, stumpy tails or no tail at all. All are vegetarian or omnivorous, eating mainly fruit, buds and leaves, but they take insects and other animals when they can.

Apes are mostly larger and heavier than monkeys, with no tails. One family, the gibbons (see pages 30-31), use their long arms and legs to swing through the forest canopy. Gorillas, chimpanzees and orang-utans, together called the 'great apes' (pages 32-39), are less agile. Though all can climb, gorillas and chimpanzees forage mainly on the ground and in the lower branches of trees, sometimes walking upright, but usually crouching or moving on all four limbs. Orang-utans spend more of their lives in the trees.

Humans are similar in size and shape to the great apes, and of course live on the ground. Where the apes are mostly herbivorous, eating leaves and fruit, humans are omnivores, eating a wide range of plant and animal food. Unlike monkeys and apes, they stand and walk upright, leaving their arms and hands free for other actions and activities. The illustration shows an early form of human being, smaller than modern humans, who lived in China, Indonesia, North and East Africa and possibly Europe. This species, which used tools and fire, died out about half a million years ago.

Pygmy chimpanzee

Patas monkey

Patas monkey

STANDING UPRIGHT

Monkeys often sit up on their haunches, but do not usually stand or walk upright. Apes, including gibbons, can stand upright, and most can walk more or less upright, if only for a few steps. Only humans stand, walk and run entirely on their hindlegs. When danger threatens, monkeys and gibbons swing off through the trees, the great apes race away on all fours, but humans stay upright, striding and running in a way that is all their own.

Pygmy chimpanzee

Lowland gorilla

Early human

RELATIONSHIPS

The three primates illustrated (left) are of the more advanced kind – the ones that biologists group in the suborder Anthropoidea (page 8). Patas monkeys are just one of about 130 living species of monkeys. You will find out more about them on pages 24-25. Pygmy chimpanzees are one of 10 species of apes (see pages 34-35). Early humans are dealt with more fully on pages 40-41.

Where they live

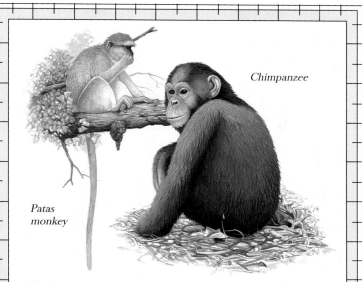

Chimpanzee

Patas monkey

Monkeys spend most of their time in the trees (left) while apes live mostly on the ground (right)

Monkeys generally live in the trees of tropical or subtropical forests, more among the branches than on the ground. Some species – such as the Patas monkey – feed on open grassland at the forest edge, never straying far from the safety of trees. Patas monkeys are found across central Africa from Senegal in the west to Sudan in the east, and as far south as Tanzania.

Apes, too, live in or near tropical forests. Larger and heavier than monkeys, they spend more of their time on the ground, but still climb trees for food and safety. Pygmy chimpanzees live in the dense rainforests of the Democratic Republic of Congo, in central Africa, close to the meeting of the Congo and Lualaba rivers.

The fossil record tells us that early humans lived in forests and grassland, spent most of their lives on the ground, and walked upright rather than on all fours. The earliest human bones have been found in Africa. From there, humans later spread to Europe, Asia and the rest of the world (see page 41).

OLD WORLD, NEW WORLD

The Old World is the continental mass that includes Europe, Asia and Africa. The New World is North and South America. When people were emigrating from Europe to North America in the 1800s, they spoke of leaving the old world to find a new life in the new world. The names have stuck, and biologists use the terms when they are describing the different kinds of plant and animal communities on either side of the Atlantic Ocean.

The Old World has about 80 species of monkeys, the New World about 50 species, but they belong to different families, and none of the species lives in both. Apes occur only in the Old World, some in Africa, others in Asia.

NEW WORLD MONKEYS 1

Marmosets and tamarins – squirrel-like monkeys of the South American forests.

FACT FILE

COMMON MARMOSET

Suborder:	Anthropoidea
Family:	Callitrichidae
Scientific name:	*Callithrix jacchus*
Colour:	Variable, grey to dark brown, with pale face and ear tufts
Weight:	330 g (12 oz)
Length, head and body:	20 cm (8 in)
Habitat:	Tropical wet or dry rainforest and savannah
Range:	Amazon river river basin, Brazil

COTTONTOP TAMARIN

Suborder:	Anthropoidea
Family:	Callitrichidae
Scientific name:	*Saguinus oedipus*
Colour:	Reddish-brown back and hindquarters, white underparts, forelimbs and crest
Weight:	360 g (13 oz)
Length, head and body:	20 cm (8 in)
Habitat:	Tropical rainforest
Range:	Northern Amazon river basin, Colombia

LION TAMARIN

Suborder:	Anthropoidea
Family:	Callitrichidae
Scientific name:	*Leontopithecus rosalia*
Colour:	Golden-brown
Weight:	650 g (1 lb 7 oz)
Length, head and body:	35 cm (14 in)
Habitat:	Tropical rainforest
Range:	Southern Brazil

Marmosets are small, fast-moving monkeys, furry and compact, with furry tails one-and-a-half times as long as their bodies. Similar in build to lemurs, and often likened to squirrels, they race up and down the trunks and along the branches of forest trees. If you see one, there are usually several more close at hand. However, they are easily scared, and their dull grey and brown fur is good camouflage.

Marmosets feed mainly on insects, spiders and other small animals. They use their chisel-shaped front teeth to gouge holes in tree trunks and then they lap up the sticky sap. Most of their fingers and toes are armed with claws. Only the big toes have flattened nails.

Slightly larger than marmosets, tamarins are more brightly coloured, with longer, sleeker fur.

Their canine teeth are long and sharp, like those of a dog or cat. These, too, are lively, squirrel-like animals that forage by day in dense patches of forest. The reddish-brown cottontop tamarin gets its name from the prominent tufts of white fur immediately above its eyes. Lion tamarins have long golden-brown fur, with an even longer swept-back mane covering the head and shoulders. These are now among the rarest of all monkeys (see page 43).

Lion tamarin

Cottontop tamarin

Emperor tamarin

FAMILY LIFE

Marmosets live in small family groups, often including a male and female with one or two growing young, sometimes in the company of two or three others, perhaps the young of previous years. Tamarins usually move in larger groups of up to 40 individuals.

Within their groups, both marmosets and tamarins constantly call to each other, forage together, and sit together on branches, squabbling mildly and grooming each other's fur in a companionable way. Young are born at any time of the year. Mothers usually give birth to twins, which both parents carry on their backs for several weeks, until they are strong enough to keep up with the group. The young reach independence at four to five months. Females are ready to mate again within three or four weeks of giving birth, so each pair may produce more than one litter per year.

RELATIONSHIPS

The 50 or so species of New World monkeys are listed by some biologists in one family, the Cebidae. Others separate the marmosets and tamarins into a family of their own, the Callitrichidae, and that is how we divide them here. The eight species of marmosets and 13 of tamarins are all smaller and in some ways less specialized than the rest of the New World monkeys.

Where they live

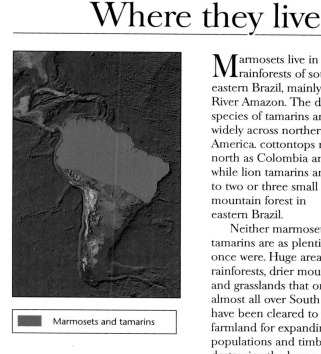

Marmosets and tamarins

Almost all-white lion tamarin

Marmosets live in the dense rainforests of southern and eastern Brazil, mainly south of the River Amazon. The different species of tamarins are scattered widely across northern South America. cottontops range as far north as Colombia and Panama, while lion tamarins are restricted to two or three small areas of mountain forest in eastern Brazil.

Neither marmosets nor tamarins are as plentiful as they once were. Huge areas of rainforests, drier mountain forests and grasslands that once spread almost all over South America have been cleared to provide farmland for expanding human populations and timber for export, destroying the homes and feeding territories of many kinds of wild animals, including primates. Several species are severely reduced, and likely to disappear as the clearance continues (see page 42-43).

GROOMING

When monkeys of all kinds have nothing more urgent to do, they sit together and groom each other's fur. Using their fingers and teeth, they comb and pick out particles – dried skin, seeds, bits of twig – and parasites such as lice. This benefits both. The one grooming seems to enjoy the activity, and the one who is groomed ends up with cleaner fur and skin. However, it is also a form of bonding, in which two individuals come close and relax in each other's company, without wasting energy in distrust or aggression.

NEW WORLD AND OLD WORLD MONKEYS

New World and Old World monkeys differ physically in several small but important ways. The most obvious difference is in their faces. New World monkeys tend to have flat noses, with widely separated nostrils that open sideways. Those of the Old World have longer noses, sometimes with a central ridge, and always with the nostrils close together and opening forward like a dog's, or downwards like our own. Old World monkeys often have hard bare patches on their buttocks. New World monkeys never have this feature.

Common marmoset

THE SMALLEST MONKEYS

Pygmy marmosets *(Cebuella pygmaea)* are similar to common marmosets, but much smaller. Smallest of all the monkeys, fully grown pygmy marmosets are only about 17 cm (7 in) long. They live in the forests of the northwestern Amazon basin, from northern Bolivia to eastern Ecuador.

NEW WORLD MONKEYS 2

Capuchins, douroucoulis and titi monkeys.

FACT FILE

BLACK-CAPPED CAPUCHIN

Suborder:	Anthropoidea
Family:	Cebidae
Scientific name:	*Cebus apella*
Colour:	Dark brown-grey, with black cap, forearms, lower legs and tail
Weight:	Male 3.5kg (7lb 9oz), female 3kg (6lb 10oz)
Length, head and body:	Male 50 cm (20 in), female 45 cm (18 in)
Habitat:	Tropical and mountain rainforest
Range:	Mainly Brazil

DOUROUCOULI

Suborder:	Anthropoidea
Family:	Cebidae
Scientific name:	*Aotus trivirgatus*
Colour:	Grey-brown back and flanks, golden yellow underparts; white face with dark muzzle
Weight:	1 kg (2 lb 3 oz)
Length, head and body:	35 cm (14 in)
Habitat:	Tropical forests
Range:	Panama south to Uruguay

WHITE-HANDED TITI

Suborder:	Anthropoidea
Family:	Cebidae
Scientific name:	*Callicebus torquatus*
Colour:	Dark reddish-brown, with pale white or orange throat, white or pale yellow hands
Weight:	1 kg (2 lb 3 oz)
Length, head and body:	40 cm (16 in)
Habitat:	Tropical rainforest
Range:	Northwestern South America

RELATIONSHIPS

These are some members of the great family of cebid monkeys of South America. The following pages show more species from different branches of the family. There are four species of capuchin monkeys, all rather similar, and three species of titi monkeys, which are closely related to the capuchins. There is just one species of douroucouli – strange monkeys with large eyes and mournful voices, that sleep by day and hunt at night.

CAPUCHIN MONKEYS gained their name from the pointed crest on the back of their head, which looks like a monk's cowl, or 'capuche'. The four species have different arrangements of tufted fur around the head, giving them different facial expressions. These are lively, active little animals – closer to everyone's idea of a monkey than marmosets and tamarins. Black-capped capuchins live in bands of a dozen or more at all levels of the rainforest. They feed mainly on nuts, fruit and leaves, but also hunt actively for insects, frogs, lizards and birds.

Douroucoulis are more solitary and solemn. Where most monkeys are active by day, these forage at night. Shine a torch in the trees after dark, and you may see huge, owl-like eyes blinking in a flat, grey and white face – hence the alternative name, 'owl monkeys'. Foraging – for insects, spiders, birds and small mammals – is carried out as quietly as possible. Between bouts of hunting, the males call with an extraordinary range of howls and hoots produced from a resonating chamber in the throat. The calls – from which they get their name – help to keep other douroucoulis at a distance, so they avoid hunting over the same territory.

Titi monkeys, like capuchins, are lively and active by day. While some inhabit tangled, lowland jungles and wet, even swampy, rainforest, the white-handed titis shown here seem to prefer drier, upland forests, at all levels from near-ground to tree-tops. These are also called 'widow monkeys', because widows in the countries where they live often wear white gloves and scarves as a sign of mourning. Titis feed mainly on nuts and fruit, but also hunt insects and small reptiles, birds and mammals. Intelligent and inquisitive, they use their hands, which have opposable thumbs (see page 19), to grasp and examine objects.

White-throated Capuchin monkey grasping a snake

Where they live

FAMILY LIFE

Capuchin monkeys live in family groups of up to a dozen, sometimes joining to form troops of 40 or more. They live in large territories, which they patrol every day, with regular feeding and watering stations. They breed throughout the year, with each female giving birth to just one baby at a time. Both parents look after the baby.

Douroucoulis and titi monkeys are less sociable, living alone or in small family groups of three or four. Each group holds a feeding territory of a few square kilometres, from which it excludes neighbours as much as possible by calling, and occasionally by threatening or fighting. They, too, produce one baby at a time and both parents care for it for about a year.

White-throated capuchin

PREDATORS

New World monkeys that live near the ground are in constant danger from snakes and several different kinds of wild forest cats. Those that forage higher in trees are sometimes taken by eagles. Another important predator is man. Some of these monkeys are good to eat. Living in groups provides some protection – there are more pairs of eyes to watch and more ears to listen for signs of danger.

White-handed titi

Douroucouli

Capuchins are widely distributed in rainforests on both sides of the Andes, from Panama in the north to northern Argentina, and they are also found in Trinidad. Black-capped capuchins live in the Amazon basin, in both the hot, damp jungles bordering the rivers and in drier mountain forests up to about 3,000 m (10,000 ft) above sea level. Within this range live several subspecies, which have slightly different colouring and adaptations for living in different climates, with different foods available to them.

Douroucoulis, too, have a wide distribution, from northern Panama to Argentina and Uruguay. Titi monkeys live in the Amazon basin, particularly south of the great river and among its headwaters. White-handed titis occur mostly on mountain slopes along the eastern flank of the Andes.

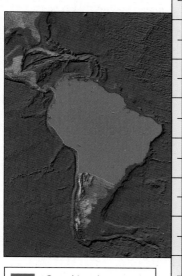

Capuchins, douroucoulis and titi monkeys

Dusky titi

Douroucouli

PREHENSILE TAILS

Most South American monkeys have long, muscular prehensile tails – tails with a tip that can curl round and grasp. Some swing by their tails, but the kinds shown here use them mainly for grasping and balance. Capuchins can pick up nuts, peanut-sized or larger, in the tips of their tails, throw them in the air and catch them by hand. Titis crouch on a branch with all four feet close together, like a cat, and the tail hanging down behind. The heavy tail, almost as long as the body, acts as a counterweight, helping to hold the body upright, or the tip can wrap around a nearby branch for support.

When two titis – a mother and half-grown young, for example – sit close together, they may intertwine their tails like a rope. They seem to feel safer holding on in that way.

NEW WORLD MONKEYS 3

Squirrel, howler, saki, uakari, spider and woolly monkeys.

FACT FILE

BLACK HOWLER MONKEY

Suborder:	Anthropoidea
Family:	Cebidae
Scientific name:	*Alouatta caraya*
Colour:	Females and young grey-brown, males entirely black
Weight:	6.5 kg (14 lb)
Length, head and body:	Males 20 cm (8 in)
Habitat:	Tropical rainforest
Range:	Central South America

COMMON SQUIRREL MONKEY

Suborder:	Anthropoidea
Family:	Cebidae
Scientific name:	*Saimiri sciureus*
Colour:	Greenish-fawn back, paler below, white face with black muzzle
Weight:	Male 1 kg (2lb 3oz), female 700 g (1lb 8oz)
Length, head and body:	Males 35 cm (14 in), females 28 cm (11 in)
Habitat:	Tropical rainforest
Range:	North and central South America

BLACK-HANDED SPIDER MONKEY

Suborder:	Anthropoidea
Family:	Cebidae
Scientific name:	*Ateles geoffroyi*
Colour:	Brown, with pale underparts, darker hands and feet
Weight:	7.5 kg (16 lb 8 oz)
Length, head and body:	50 cm (20 in)
Habitat:	Tropical forest
Range:	From Mexico to Panama

Howlers, among the largest and heaviest of the South American monkeys, live in troops of up to 20. They prefer large trees with strong branches, and each troop needs plenty of room to feed. While several kinds of monkeys gibber and shriek to announce their presence and keep others away, howlers have specially developed bony voice-boxes that enable them to howl or roar in chorus. Males are particularly noisy, their voices carrying for hundreds of metres through the trees. Groups roar especially around sunrise, and when they meet other troops. They feed mainly on young leaves and fruit.

Squirrel monkeys, smallest of the cebid monkeys, live in forests up to about 300 m (1,000 ft) above sea level, rarely higher. Smaller and quieter than howlers, they live in groups of 30-40, and feed on a variety of buds, fruit, insects and other small animals.

Spider monkeys are slender, with long arms and legs. Their fingers and toes are also extended, and they have no thumbs. Woolly monkeys are similar but fatter, with longer, denser fur. Heaviest of all South American monkeys are woolly spider monkeys (*Brachyteles arachnoides*), which weigh up to 12 kg (26 lb). Spider and woolly monkeys leap and swing through the trees, holding on with hands, feet and prehensile tail.

Saki and uakari monkeys, though closely related, are strikingly different in appearance. Both have long fur and bushy tails, but sakis have dense manes and facial hair, while uakaris are almost completely bald, with bare faces either black or brilliant red. They leap – almost fly – through the tree-tops, feeding mainly on fruit and nuts.

White-faced saki

Howler monkeys in chorus

FAMILY LIFE

These are all sociable species of monkeys, living in troops that travel and feed together in close company. Often a troop consists of a core of females with babies and young, with loosely attached attendant males. Mature males lead the troops through the forest, and make most noise when they encounter rival troops. The males are ready to mate with the females as they come on heat, but take no part in rearing the young. The gestation period (from mating to birth) is 7 to 8 months. Females give birth to one baby at a time, carrying them for several weeks on their backs.

Common woolly monkey and young

RELATIONSHIPS

These are all monkeys that live in the tropical forests of Central or South America. Biologists cannot agree on how many species there are of each, or how to classify them. There are usually thought to be five or six species of howlers, and two of squirrel monkeys. Sakis and uakaris, probably closely related to each other, have three or four species each. Spider and woolly monkeys are close relatives, too, with about seven species in total.

Black-handed spider monkey

Common squirrel monkey

Where they live

Howler monkeys reach their northern limit in southern Mexico, and their southern limit in Argentina, Paraguay and eastern Brazil. Black howlers live in central South America, in parts of southern Brazil, Paraguay and Bolivia. Squirrel monkeys extend northwards from this region to the north coast of South America, and on into western Panama and Costa Rica. Spider monkeys, too, are widespread from southern Mexico to the Amazon basin. Woolly monkeys, uakaris and saki monkeys have more restricted ranges within the Amazon basin.

In many of these areas several species of monkeys overlap, sometimes competing for food, sometimes feeding side by side but on different kinds of food growing in the same area. So rich are these forests that there is usually plenty for all. Though monkeys tend to be hostile to other troops within their own species, they often mix quite amicably with troops of

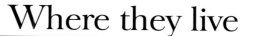

	Squirrel, howler, saki, uakari, spider and woolly monkeys

different species. Each species quickly learns to respond to the alarm calls of the other. Even if they are competing for food, they benefit by the extra pairs of ears and eyes on the lookout for danger.

Red uakari

Spider monkey

OPPOSABLE THUMBS

When you hold an object with one hand, your fingers and thumbs take opposite sides and grasp it between them. You cannot do the same with your toes. Big toes are not opposable in the same way as thumbs. Few other animals have opposable thumbs. Though in nearly all primates the thumbs are separate from the fingers and almost as long, not all primates can use them to grasp.

This is a simple but very

important feature that allows some primates – including ourselves – to hold objects, turn them over, roll them about, examine them and even take them to pieces.

Some monkeys without opposable thumbs, such as howlers, sakis and uakaris, pick up small objects between their second and third fingers. Try it, and you will find that you can pick things up, but not examine them half as well as you can with an opposable thumb.

MACAQUES, BARBARY 'APES' AND MANGABEYS

Old World monkeys of Asia, Gibraltar and Africa.

FACT FILE

JAPANESE MACAQUE

Suborder:	Anthropoidea
Family:	Cercopithecidae
Subfamily:	Cercopithecinae
Scientific name:	*Macaca fuscata*
Colour:	Grey-brown fur, pink face
Weight:	8-18 kg (18-40 lb)
Length, head and body:	50-60 cm (20-24 in)
Habitat:	Forest and open ground
Range:	Japan

BARBARY 'APE'

Suborder:	Anthropoidea
Family:	Cercopithecidae
Subfamily:	Cercopithecinae
Scientific name:	*Macaca sylvanus*
Colour:	Reddish-brown
Weight:	11-15 kg (24-33 lb]
Length, head and body:	50-60 cm (20-24 in)
Habitat:	Forest, scrub and grassland
Range:	Morocco, Algeria, Gibraltar

WHITE-COLLARED MANGABEY

Suborder:	Anthropoidea
Family:	Cercopithecidae
Subfamily:	Cercopithecinae
Scientific name:	*Cercocebus torquatus*
Colour:	Grey, with white collar, dark face and white eyebrows
Weight:	10 kg (22 lb)
Length, head and body:	60 cm (24 in)
Habitat:	Tropical rainforest
Range:	Ghana, Nigeria, Cameroon and Gabon

MACAQUE IS THE GENERAL name for about 16 species of monkeys that live across northern Africa and Asia. They live in all kinds of environments, from tropical forests to cold mountain scrub, some almost entirely in trees, others mainly on the ground. The tree-living species tend to have long tails, the ground-living ones short tails or none at all. They eat whatever food is around, from fruit and shoots in the forest to farm produce and refuse in cities.

Japanese macaques live further north than any other monkeys. They have bare red faces, but their bodies are clothed with thick grey-brown fur that keeps them warm in the coldest of winters. They are active even in snowy weather, when they often bathe in Japan's numerous hot springs. Unlike most monkeys, they are good swimmers. The animals live mainly on the ground and are largely vegetarian. They form large troops, each strictly ruled by an old male.

Barbary 'apes' are not really apes. They have been misnamed; in fact they are tail-less monkeys that live in scattered groups in the mountains of northwest Africa. A small population inhabits the Rock of Gibraltar, just across the Strait of Gibraltar on the southern tip of Spain (see opposite page).

Mangabeys are slender monkeys of African tropical forests, with tails longer than their head and body. Some are black or dark brown. Others, like the one illustrated, are splashed with patches of bright colour. Their white eyebrows flash when they are frightened or threatening. They feed both in the trees and on the ground, mainly on nuts and fruit.

Barbary 'apes', a species of macaque – the baby will soon lose its dark colour

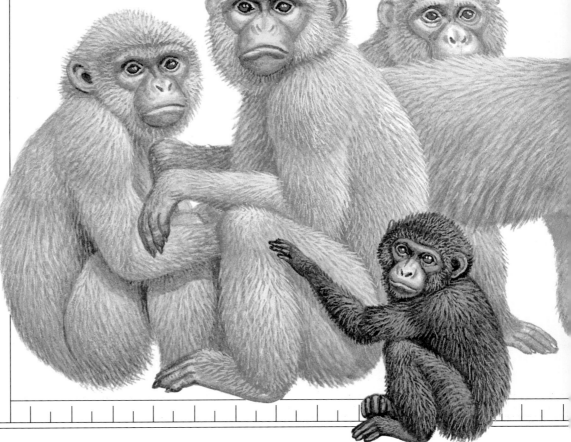

Rhesus macaques

FAMILY LIFE

Macaques live in troops ranging in size from a few dozen to hundreds – in general, the better the feeding, the bigger the troop. In the tropics, where food is usually plentiful, they breed at any time of year. In Japan, China and other areas where winters can be intensely cold, they mate in autumn, producing their single babies during early summer.

Mangabeys also live in troops, but usually smaller ones, often of only one or up to three or four males and nine to a dozen females with young. They breed throughout the year, the females producing single babies, which cling to their fur and ride on their backs. Group living helps to protect them from ground predators, especially leopards and other cats that try to creep up unseen.

RELATIONSHIPS

Old World monkeys are all included in the single family Cercopithecidae, but fall into two subfamily groups. The subfamily Cercopithecinae includes the macaques, mangabeys, guenons, baboons, mandrills and their relatives. The subfamily Colobinae includes the colobus and leaf monkeys and their relatives.

Macaques include rhesus monkeys, Barbary 'apes', which are not apes at all, and many other well-known species. The four kinds of mangabeys are African cousins, larger and heavier, but similar to macaques and closely related to them.

Agile mangabey

Where they live

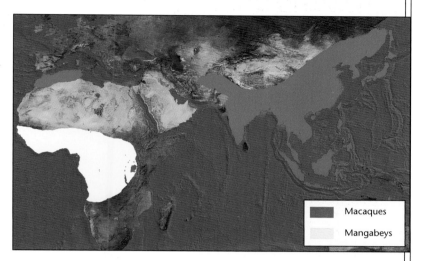

Macaques
Mangabeys

Macaques have the widest distribution of any group of monkeys, though the different species occupy narrower areas within this span. They are found in northern Africa and across Asia to Indonesia and Japan. Small-to-medium-sized monkeys, they have many local names. From northern India to China they are rhesus monkeys, in southern India bonnet macaques, in Sri Lanka toque monkeys, in Indonesia crab-eating monkeys and in northern Africa and Gibraltar Barbary 'apes'. Japanese macaques have a relatively limited distribution in Japan itself. Mangabeys live in the tropical forests of west and central Africa. White-collared mangabeys are found in a limited area of southern Nigeria, Cameroon and Gabon.

MONKEYS FOR MEDICAL RESEARCH

Rhesus monkeys, small and relatively easy to keep in captivity, have for many years been exported from India to medical laboratories all over the world. Though laboratories have bred them too, it has generally been easier and cheaper to buy them from suppliers, who in turn buy them from hunters and trappers. Similar to humans in some of their physiology and body chemistry, rhesus monkeys have contributed to many important medical discoveries, including blood-typing and the development of vaccines.

People concerned with animal welfare want to stop the trade, claiming that it is cruel, and that thousands of monkeys die each year before they ever reach the laboratories. Researchers point to the progress made, and the number of human lives saved, by having rhesus and other monkeys available for research.

Should monkeys be caught, traded and used in this way? What do you think?

MACAQUES OF GIBRALTAR

The Barbary macaques on the British colony of Gibraltar are the only wild monkeys in Europe. Their ancestors may have included the last remnants of a much larger European population, but numbers today are

boosted from time to time by imports from Africa. According to a centuries-old tradition, if the 'apes' leave the Rock of Gibraltar, Britain will lose its colony. So the British government looks after them. Though wild, they are in the care of the British garrison, and are a pampered tourist attraction.

Japanese macaque – these hardy monkeys are good swimmers and bathe in hot springs even when it snows

AFRICAN GROUND-LIVING MONKEYS

Baboons, mandrills, drills and geladas.

FACT FILE

HAMADRYAS BABOON

Suborder:	Anthropoidea
Family:	Cercopithecidae
Subfamily:	Cercopithecinae
Scientific name:	*Papio hamadryas*
Colour:	Brown, males with grey cape, red face and buttocks
Weight:	Males 15 kg (33 lb), females 10 kg (22 lb)
Length, head and body:	75 cm (30 in)
Habitat:	Desert scrub, grassland
Range:	Northeastern Africa, Arabia

MANDRILL

Suborder:	Anthropoidea
Family:	Cercopithecidae
Subfamily:	Cercopithecinae
Scientific name:	*Mandrillus sphinx*
Colour:	Grey-brown back, paler underparts, blue cheeks, red nose, blue buttocks
Weight:	Males 25 kg (55 lb), females 12 kg (26 lb)
Length, head and body:	70-80 cm (28-31 in)
Habitat:	Rainforest edge
Range:	Cameroon, Congo Republic, Gabon

DRILL

Suborder:	Anthropoidea
Family:	Cercopithecidae
Subfamily:	Cercopithecinae
Scientific name:	*Mandrillus leucophaeus*
Colour:	Dark brown body, black face, white beard, blue buttocks
Weight:	Males 45 kg (100 lb), females smaller
Length, head and body:	70 cm (28 in)
Habitat:	Rainforest edge
Range:	Nigeria, Cameroon

GELADA

Suborder:	Anthropoidea
Family:	Cercopithecidae
Subfamily:	Cercopithecinae
Scientific name:	*Theropithecus gelada*
Colour:	Dark to paler brown body, cape over shoulders, red skin on neck and buttocks
Weight:	Males 20 kg (44 lb), females 14 kg (31 lb)
Length, head and body:	70 cm (28 in)
Habitat:	Open grassland, scrub
Range:	Ethiopia

THESE ARE ALL AFRICAN ground-living monkeys. Some live in forests, others in open woodland or scrub, others again in grassland and semidesert where there is not a tree for miles. Females and young spend more time in the trees, while heavier males use their weight to push through dense undergrowth. When danger threatens, they all climb nimbly, shinning up trees or cliffs faster than snakes or cats can follow, and barking loudly from the top to warn the world of predators. They sleep in high places at night. During the day they forage on the ground, scrabbling and searching for their favourite foods – seeds, nuts, grass, new shoots, fresh leaves, insects, birds and small mammals.

Though the name 'hamadryas' comes from a word meaning 'tree-spirit', hamadryas baboons live in semidesert areas of northeast Africa and southern Arabia, mainly in dry, open woodland and grassy plains. The ancient Egyptians regarded them as wise and sacred, training them to live in their houses and temples, and preserving them as mummies after death. Other species of baboons live in similar dry habitats, extending over much of southern and eastern Africa.

Mandrills and drills are heavyweight baboons of tropical forests. They live mainly on the ground, but take to the sturdy lower branches of trees for travel and safety. Both have drab, grey-brown body fur. In drills this extends to the face, enlivened by a smart white

Hamadryas baboon

Gelada

beard and collar. Mandrills by contrast are brightly decorated, with golden beard and collar, blue grooved cheeks and vivid red nose. Both species have bright sky-blue buttocks.

Geladas, too, are heavyweights. They live on treeless plateaus of Ethiopia. Though their fur is drab, they have patches of pink wattled skin on the chest and buttocks, which brighten in females that are ready to mate. At rest, the face is dark, but a male threatening his neighbours exposes vivid white eyebrows and peels back his upper lip, showing pink gums and a formidable set of teeth. Geladas feed mainly on grass, which they pluck by hand, and on fruit, roots, flowers and leaves.

Drill

Mandrill

FAMILY LIFE

Baboons, mandrills, drills and geladas live in troops of up to about 20, dominated by a single old male but including several females, young and immature males, which patrol widely over extensive feeding

Baby baboon eating fruit

areas. At times these band together into much larger groups, perhaps to share a sudden super-abundance of fruit or grass. Troops often congregate at night among trees and on cliffs where they can sleep safely.

These species all breed throughout the year, with no marked seasons. Females have menstrual cycles of four to five weeks, often indicating the mid-point of the cycle – the few days when they are most fertile – by a change in colour of the buttocks. Gestation takes between 24 and 28 weeks, producing single babies, rarely twins.

Where they live

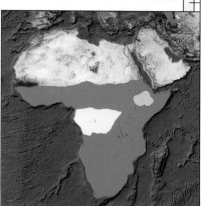

Baboons are widespread throughout Africa south of the Sahara, extending into the western tip of Arabia. Hamadryas baboons occupy only the dry northeastern corner of this range, including parts of Sudan, Ethiopia, Somalia and Yemen.

Mandrills live in the rainforests of West Africa – in Cameroon, Equatorial Guinea, Gabon and Congo Republic. Drills live a little further north, in northern Cameroon and southern Nigeria, and on the nearby island of Bioko. Geladas live only on high grasslands in the northern and central mountains of Ethiopia.

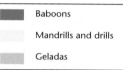

■	Baboons
□	Mandrills and drills
▨	Geladas

Male mandrill snarling

RELATIONSHIPS

The five species of baboons, the drill, the mandrill and the gelada are closely related and biologists often put them all in a single genus. They are all strongly built and quite powerful animals with long, dog-like muzzles. Although they feed mainly on plants, baboons living in open country often catch hares and small antelopes. Their big canine teeth are dangerous weapons and even a leopard will hesitate to attack a troop of baboons.

GROUND LIVING

A gelada standing upright

We know baboons and their kin are not immediate ancestors of man. But they have taken the first important step that more direct ancestors must have taken – coming down from the trees, and starting to find ways of living on open ground, away from the forest edge.

They walk or scramble on all fours, using their fingers as toes, and cannot walk upright as we can. But when feeding they sit back on their haunches, freeing their hands for plucking, grasping, digging, and examining what they have found. This is a second important step, leading to a clearer understanding of the world around them.

SOME AFRICAN FOREST MONKEYS

Guenons, talapoins and patas monkeys.

MEDIUM-SIZED MONKEYS, with long limbs and a tail longer than the head and body, guenons live in troops of a dozen or more that move through the forest in a constant, chattering search for food and excitement. They are among the most colourful of monkeys, basically brown or grey, but decorated with red, white or golden fur, and flashes of red, white or blue skin. These decorations are found particularly on the head, face and neck, and on the rump, buttocks and genital regions – the areas that show when they are active in the trees. Males are usually larger than females.

Moustached guenons have a striking colour scheme of black-tinged brown fur, with reddish-brown on the rump and tail, white underparts and multi-coloured face. The diana monkey, also a guenon, has a distinctive beard. Other guenons include species with white noses and ear-tufts, golden cheeks, blue faces, red noses and ears, and many more variations. By these features, members of the different species can quickly recognize each other on sight.

Talapoin monkeys, the smallest of the Old World monkeys, live in low swampy forest, never far from water. They often feed and sleep in the low canopy overhanging rivers and lakes. While all monkeys can swim when they need to, talapoins seem to regard swimming as part of their way of life, leaping into the water to avoid predators, to catch food, or possibly just to cool down.

Patas monkeys (for Fact File, see page 12) prefer dry forest, savanna, scrub, and even sandy desert. Long-tailed and long-limbed like guenons, they live mainly on the ground, climbing trees or cliffs only for safety or to see farther. Unlike guenons they can stand and walk upright on their hindlegs, using the tail as a prop. If chased by a predator, they run on all fours. They have been clocked at 50 km/h (30 mph) and more. Patas monkeys can outrun most small cats. By twisting, turning, and eventually climbing to safety, they can even outsmart lions, leopards and cheetahs.

Moustached guenon

Talapoin

Where they live

Patas monkeys drinking at a pool

RELATIONSHIPS

Guenon is a general name for about 20 species of monkeys grouped in the genus *Cercopithecus* – after which the family and subfamily are named. These are Africa's commonest monkeys, the different species occurring in a wide variety of forests from dripping jungle to dry woodlands and savanna. Talapoins are similar to guenons, but smaller, with a marked preference for swamp forest. Patas monkeys round off the group, clearly related to guenons, but ground-living.

Guenons occupy a wide swathe of central and southern Africa. Most widespread is the green, or vervet, monkey, *Cercopithecus aethiops*, which is found from the southern edge of the Sahara to the Sudan and Ethiopia, and south to Cape Province. Moustached guenons have a comparatively limited range in the forests of Gabon, Cameroon, Central African Republic and Congo Republic, north of the River Congo. Other species are scattered across central Africa from the west coast to the Rift Valley.

The talapoins inhabit the lowland forests of western central Africa, from Cameroon in the north to Angola in the south. Patas monkeys live in the dry savanna zone – between deserts to the north and forests to the south – that runs across northern Africa from Senegal to Sudan, ranging south into Uganda, Kenya and Tanzania.

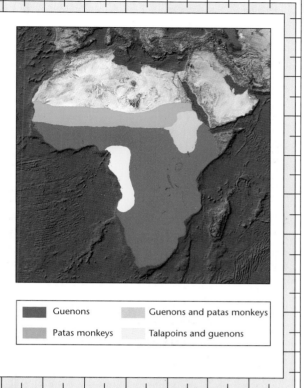

■ Guenons	■ Guenons and patas monkeys
■ Patas monkeys	■ Talapoins and guenons

FAMILY LIFE

Guenons live in troops of between 12 and 20, each centred on a territory but feeding in larger home ranges where several groups may overlap.

Troops include two or three adult males, four or five adult females, mostly with babies, and as many immature young. Members of the troop sleep together at night and forage together by day,

Talapoin mother with young

maintaining a constant watch for predators. On the ground their main enemies are snakes and cats. In the tree-tops they fall prey to eagles.

Guenons breed at any time of the year. For the first few weeks of life, the baby clings to its mother's fur, then later rides piggy-back until it can keep up with the troop.

Talapoins have a similar social life, though their troops usually number 50-100 or more. Females give birth to unusually large offspring, weighing one-fifth as much as the mother.

Patas monkeys run in troops of up to 12, each dominated by a single adult male. Males in this species are notably bigger than females. Troop leaders use their bulk to threaten and keep away rival males.

Diana monkey

DIVIDING THE FOREST

Tropical forests have distinct layers. The tallest trees form a high canopy around 45 m (150 ft). Lesser trees form a lower canopy around 30 m (100 ft). Below them is a layer of shrubs and a tangle of undergrowth. The Diana monkey (pictured left) feeds high in the tallest trees, the moustached guenon at much lower levels, and others species in the middle layers. However, nearly all climb to bed at night, seeking the comparative safety of the higher branches.

Patas monkey on a branch

COLOBUS MONKEYS OF AFRICA

Leaf-eating monkeys of African forests.

FACT FILE

SATANIC BLACK COLOBUS MONKEY

Suborder:	Anthropoidea
Family:	Cercopithecidae
Subfamily:	Colobinae
Scientific name:	*Colobus satanas*
Colour:	Black back, head, face
Weight:	10 kg (22 lb)
Length, head and body:	70 cm (28 in)
Habitat:	Tropical forest
Range:	Cameroon, Equatorial Guinea, Gabon and Congo Republic

GUINEA RED COLOBUS MONKEY

Suborder:	Anthropoidea
Family:	Cercopithecidae
Subfamily:	Colobinae
Scientific name:	*Procolobus badius*
Colour:	Reddish-brown back and head, pale cream underparts
Weight:	8 kg (18 lb)
Length, head and body:	60 cm (24 in)
Habitat:	Tropical forest and savanna
Range:	Senegal, Gambia and Ghana

RELATIONSHIPS

Colobus monkeys are medium-sized African forest monkeys, reddish-brown or black, with big stomachs and spindly limbs and tails. The name 'colobus', meaning mutilated or deformed, refers to their hands, in which the thumbs are very small or absent. Biologists do not all agree on how many kinds of colobus monkeys there are, but there are probably four black colobus species and five red colobus species. Black colobus monkeys have three stomach chambers, but red colobus monkeys have four. For this reason, they are now usually placed in separate genera – Colobus for the black and Procolobus for the red.

COLOBUS MONKEYS are slightly bigger than guenons, but quieter, more placid, and less likely to create disturbance. In a treeful of monkeys, where groups of both are present, you are likely to notice the guenons immediately, from their lively movements and chattering. Only gradually will you see or hear colobus monkeys among them. Colobus monkeys lack the brilliant colours of guenons. Some are all black or starkly black and white, others are reddish-brown, while olive colobus are a handsome but unexciting khaki-green.

Whereas guenons feed largely on fruit and get very excited when they find a good supply, colobus monkeys feed mainly on leaves. Not having to search for their food, they spend most of their time sitting quietly in the trees eating.

The satanic black colobus shown here is one of four predominantly black monkeys. All of these have black faces ringed with white, and – except for one form – patches of long white fur on their shoulders or flanks. In some, the tails thicken to a distinct white tuft at the end. Since they were first hunted, the all-black or black-and-white furs of colobus monkeys have been in demand for ceremonial robes. Since medieval times, hundreds of thousands have been exported from central and western Africa, commanding good prices in world markets.

Red colobus monkeys are partly black but have a lot of reddish-brown fur. Their underparts are usually white or cream. Fortunately for them, red skins were valued far less than black, so red colobus monkeys were spared intensive hunting.

All the colobus monkeys spend most of their time high in the trees, browsing on leaves, and seldom bothering to descend to ground level.

Guinea red colobus monkeys

Satanic black colobus of west Africa

Where they live

Black-and-white colobus

DIGESTING TOUGH LEAVES

The evergreen leaves of the tropical forests are rather tough and not easy to digest, but the colobus monkeys have special equipment to deal with them. Their back teeth are more strongly ridged than those of the guenons, helping them to grind up the leaves better. They also have big salivary glands that produce plenty of liquid to wash the food down. Like cows and sheep, colobus monkeys have three or four stomach chambers, in which bacteria slowly break down the cellulose that forms the bulk of the leaves. Digestion takes a long time and generates a lot of gases, which the animals get rid of by frequent belching. The monkeys have to eat lots of leaves to get enough food from them, so they have to spend more time eating than most other monkeys.

FAMILY LIFE

Both the black and the red colobus monkeys live in troops, usually consisting of one or two mature males and several females. Black colobus troops of this size defend feeding territories. The males roar at dawn, dusk and at intervals throughout the day to demonstrate possession, but seldom need to defend themselves against intruders.

Troops of red colobus monkeys tend to be larger, probably by loose amalgamation of several small troops. Red colobus monkeys have smaller voice boxes than

Colobus quietly browsing up a tree

black colobus monkeys and make less noise. Large or small, colobus groups seem to live peaceably among themselves and with neighbours.

Colobus monkeys breed throughout the year. At birth, black colobus babies are covered with grey or white woolly fur, and all the females in the troop help to look after them while they are small. They gain their black and white fur at three to four months. Red colobus babies are paler than their parents, but similar in pattern, and are guarded almost exclusively by their mothers.

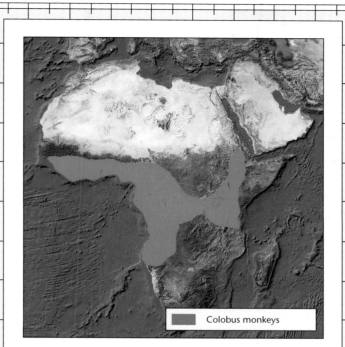

Colobus monkeys

Colobus monkeys extend in a broad belt from Guinea, on the west coast of Africa, south to Angola and northern Namibia, and east to Congo DR, Uganda, Tanzania, Kenya and Ethiopia. Satanic black colobus monkeys live in the rainforests of Cameroon, Equatorial Guinea, Gabon and Congo Republic. Guinea red colobus monkeys live only in west Africa – in the forests and on the savannas from Senegal and Gambia to Ghana.

NO THUMBS

Strong opposable thumbs (see page 19) allow some monkeys and apes – and ourselves – to grasp, turn and examine objects in our hands. Colobus monkeys, however, have only small thumbs, or none at all. Monkeys and apes that spend much of their lives brachiating (swinging from branches) usually have long fingers and long, narrow hands. In swinging, they keep their fingers together, using them as hooks. In this position a thumb just gets in the way. So brachiators are probably better off with only small thumbs.

Their ancestors may have had larger thumbs, but individuals with smaller ones fared better through the ages, and now they all have reduced thumbs.

Despite its small thumb, this colobus monkey has no trouble feeding itself

LANGURS

Leaf monkeys and proboscis monkeys of southeastern Asia.

FACT FILE

HANUMAN LANGUR

Suborder:	Anthropoidea
Family:	Cercopithecidae
Subfamily:	Colobinae
Scientific name:	*Presbytis entellus*
Colour:	Silver-grey back, pale head, black face, hands and feet
Weight:	20 kg (44 lb)
Length, head and body:	75 cm (30 in)
Habitat:	Lowland jungle to mountain forest
Range:	India, Sri Lanka, Nepal, Tibet, Bangladesh

SPECTACLED (DUSKY) LANGUR

Suborder:	Anthropoidea
Family:	Cercopithecidae
Subfamily:	Colobinae
Scientific name:	*Presbytis obscurus*
Colour:	Grey to black-brown, with head crest and prominent white eye rings
Weight:	7 kg (15 lb)
Length, head and body:	50 cm (20 in)
Habitat:	Rainforest
Range:	SE Asia, from Bangladesh to Malaysia

PROBOSCIS MONKEY

Suborder:	Anthropoidea
Family:	Cercopithecidae
Subfamily:	Colobinae
Scientific name:	*Nasalis larvatus*
Colour:	Golden-brown head and back, paler collar, limbs and underparts
Weight:	Males 20 kg (44 lb), females 10 kg (22 lb)
Length, head and body:	Males 70 cm (28 in), females 60 cm (24 in)
Habitat:	Rainforest
Range:	Borneo

RELATIONSHIPS

The slender, lively langurs are the Asian equivalents of the African colobus monkeys. Like colobuses, langurs have complex teeth, and salivary glands and stomachs that enable them to digest tough old stems, leaves and grasses, as well as softer young ones. They include about 20 species of leaf monkeys, so-called because leaves are their main food. They are commonly included in the genus *Presbytis*, a name meaning 'old woman' and possibly referring to the curiously human faces of some species. Eight other species are similar enough to be called langurs, although they are placed in different genera.

LANGURS ARE FOREST MONKEYS with long, wiry arms, legs and tails. They live in different kinds of forests from India to China and southeastern Asia. They show a curious mixture of monkey characteristics, sharing with guenons colour and decoration, and with spider and colobus monkeys the habit of brachiation − swinging by the arms, as an alternative to running and climbing through the branches.

Hanuman langurs, the common langurs of India and Sri Lanka, are among the largest of the group, and those that live in the cold mountains of Nepal and Tibet grow largest of all. Big females from the Himalayan mountain forests weigh up to 18 kg (40 lb), big males up to 23 kg (50 lb) or more. Spectacled langurs are more typical of langurs in size and weight. In all species, males are larger than females, though the difference among the smaller ones is slight.

Langurs feed on leaves and shoots, but also eat buds, flowers and softer vegetation when they become plentiful. The smaller species take most of their food directly from the trees, usually foraging in the lower canopy. Hanuman langurs spend more time on the ground. One possible reason is their weight. Another is that, throughout the Indian subcontinent, they are regarded as sacred, and so are safe from human predation. This allows them to visit villages and towns, where they can scavenge on the ground in safety, and even raid

Proboscis monkey

Spectacled langur

Mother and young proboscis monkeys

FAMILY LIFE

Langurs live in troops of varying size and composition. Some troops consist of a single male with two or three females. Often they are larger, including three or four males, a dozen or more females, and an assortment of young. They move within a territory, with one dominant male leading. Catching his troop's attention with whooping calls, he decides where they sleep and feed, and when it is time to move on, and he is the one most likely to mate successfully with the females. From time to time a young male challenges his leadership and, after a brief skirmish, may take over. Unattached males form 'bachelor' troops of their own.

Langurs communicate by calls and facial displays, but seldom fight among themselves or with other troops. Females become fertile at monthly intervals, each producing a single baby some 30 weeks after mating. Hanuman langurs have brown babies, similar to themselves but darker. Spectacled langurs have bright golden babies, in vivid contrast to their own black fur. The babies are passed around and tended by all the females in the group for several weeks, and are fed by their mothers for up to two years.

crops when other foods are scarce.

Proboscis monkeys are stoutly built langurs with handsome golden fur, a chestnut cap and a lion-like mane. Living in coastal and lowland forests, they run and leap through the trees, often hurtling about in what seems a clumsy way, sometimes swinging from both arms or hanging by one. The 'proboscis' is a long, flat nose, in females merely large but in males enormous – a huge, endearingly ugly pantomime nose, long enough to hang down over the mouth. Scientists believe it acts as a sound-chamber, giving the animals a deeper or more resonant 'honk' when they call.

Hanuman langur

Where they live

Langurs
Proboscis monkeys and other langurs

As a group, langurs extend from India in the west to Borneo in the east, and south through Malaysia, Thailand, Burma, Cambodia, Vietnam, Sumatra and Java. They also extend northwards into the Himalayas and central China.

Within this area the different species occupy much narrower ranges, though Hanuman langurs, one of the two Indian species, spread from Nepal to Sri Lanka, and spectacled langurs are at home from Bangladesh to Malaysia. They live in several different kinds of forests, from steaming lowland jungle to high, cold mountain woodlands.

Proboscis monkeys live only in Borneo, in muddy mangrove forests along coasts, estuaries and river banks, and in lowland forests close to water.

Langurs live in the forests of southeastern Asia

PLAYSCHOOL

Monkeys of all kinds stay close to their mother for the first two or three weeks, holding tight to her fur and seldom leaving her side. Soon they start to investigate the leaves and fruit that their mother is eating. They lean over her shoulder and learn by smell and taste what is good to eat. From eight to ten weeks, they are ready to explore more widely, and to start playing with each other. Young males tend to wander with other males, playing roughly with leaping, bounding and mock-fighting, and investigating strange objects with their hands. Young females stay closer to adult females, paying great attention to other babies, which from time to time they may hold and handle. Each form of play is a training for their differing roles in monkey society.

Hanuman langur with baby

FACT FILE

BLACK GIBBON

Suborder:	Anthropoidea
Family:	Hylobatidae
Scientific name:	*Hylobates concolor*
Colour:	Males, black head, body and face; females, pale head and body, black face
Weight:	5 kg (11 lb)
Length, head and body:	60 cm (24 in)
Habitat:	Tropical forest
Range:	Southern China, Laos, Cambodia, Vietnam

LAR (WHITE-HANDED) GIBBON

Suborder:	Anthropoidea
Family:	Hylobatidae
Scientific name:	*Hylobates lar*
Colour:	Black, brown or tawny, with white hands
Weight:	5 kg (11 lb)
Length, head and body:	60 cm (24 in)
Habitat:	Tropical forest
Range:	Burma, south to Sumatra and Java

SIAMANG

Suborder:	Anthropoidea
Family:	Hylobatidae
Scientific name:	*Hylobates syndactylus*
Colour:	Black with grey muzzle and beard
Weight:	10 kg (22 lb)
Length, head and body:	85 cm (33 in)
Habitat:	Tropical forest
Range:	Malay Peninsula, Sumatra

Siamang calling

APES: GIBBONS AND SIAMANGS

Swinging apes of the Asian forests.

ONE GROUP OF ASIAN APES, long-armed, broad-chested, and able to stand and walk upright, specialize in tree-living. Gibbons and siamangs are slender, graceful acrobats which, in their ability to swing through the tree-tops, are a match for the howler and spider monkeys of South America (see pages 18-19). Formerly widespread in the forests of China and beyond, these small apes are currently restricted to islands and peninsulas of southeastern Asia. With nine species, they are the most varied and versatile group of all the apes.

Unusually among monkeys and apes, male black gibbons are bright, glossy black, but females are pale, golden or grey brown, and babies are white for the first few weeks of their lives. Lar gibbons vary in colour according to where they live. Siamangs, which are larger, heavier gibbons, are mostly black.

Gibbons feed mainly on ripe fruit. Young leaves are their second choice, and they also eat insects and other invertebrates.

You usually hear gibbons long before you see them, calling to each other with curiously melodious songs. Each species has its own song. Once you know the songs and calls, you can tell which gibbons are about without seeing them.

Male and female black gibbons

Pileated gibbon

Siamang

Lar gibbon

RELATIONSHIPS

Although they climb and swing through the branches like monkeys, gibbons and siamangs are not monkeys but apes. They are like monkeys in appearance but they have no tails. They also have broader, more barrel-like chests than monkeys and they have bigger brains.

There are 13 different species of apes alive in the world today. The eight species of gibbons and the siamang, often known as the 'lesser apes', are placed in the family Hylobatidae. The four 'great apes' - the orang-utan, the gorilla and the two species of chimpanzee - make up the family Pongidae.

Gibbons and the siamang have very long arms and very powerful shoulders. Although they can walk upright on their back legs, they move through the forests mainly by swinging from hand to hand underneath the boughs. They move so quickly that they hardly seem to touch the branches. They are by far the fastest of the apes.

The great apes are generally much bigger than the gibbons and, apart from the orang-utan, spend much of their time on the ground. They can walk on their hindlegs, but usually with a stoop, and they more often walk on all fours, with their weight resting on their knuckles.

Where they live

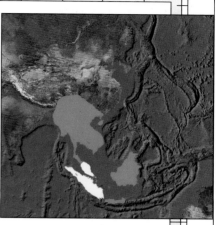

Gibbons as a group live in tall tropical forests from Assam (northeast India) and Burma in the north, through Yunnan (southern China), Thailand, Cambodia, Laos and Vietnam to Malaysia, and on through Sumatra, Java and Borneo. Throughout this wide range their forests are being felled for timber. Every year their world becomes smaller and more patchy.

Black gibbons are restricted mainly to China, Laos, eastern Cambodia and Vietnam − all areas of expanding human populations. Lar, or white-handed, gibbons have a wider distribution from mainland Burma, Thailand and the Malay Peninsula to the islands of Sumatra and Java. Siamangs are at home only in the Malay Peninsula and Sumatra.

■	Gibbons
■	Siamangs and gibbons

FAMILY LIFE

Gibbons live in small family groups, usually one adult pair with two or three juveniles. Pairs mate throughout the year, and a single baby is born after a gestation of about 30 weeks. Babies are fed on milk for over a year, then remain with their parents for five or six years. Both parents take an interest, male siamangs being especially attentive towards the youngsters, and keeping the family together.

Juvenile lar gibbon

WHAT'S IN A TAIL?

Biologists believe that apes started to evolve about 40 million years ago, from some kind of monkey that began to spend more of its time on the ground. Tails are important for monkeys that live in the trees because tails help them to maintain their balance as they scamper through the branches. The prehensile tails of some South American monkeys can even grip the branches like an extra leg. Tails are of less importance on the ground, and many ground-living monkeys have short tails: some have lost their tails altogether.

The apes also lost their tails during their evolution from monkeys, and at the same time developed long arms with very flexible hands and wrists. After living on the ground for several million years, the gibbons gradually returned to a life in the trees. Their long arms were ideal for swinging through the branches, and they became even longer as the animals became better adapted to their new life in the tree-tops. The gibbons' arms are now longer than their legs. But the gibbons never got their tails back.

THE GREAT APES

Similarities and differences among the great apes of Africa and Asia – the orang-utans, the chimpanzees and the gorillas.

RELATIONSHIPS

There is only one living species of orang-utan, with two populations that live in two separate areas of southeastern Asia. These differ from each other enough for biologists to call them separate subspecies. Similarly, there is only one species of gorilla, again with distinct populations, in this case three, forming separate subspecies. The two kinds of chimpanzees are at first sight very similar – about as similar as are the subspecies of gorilla. But they live in different areas and do not seem to interbreed. Biologists who have studied them both have no doubt that they form two distinct species.

Pygmy chimpanzee

FEEDING

The great apes, also known as anthropoid (man-like) apes, are basically vegetarian. Gorillas feed almost entirely on leaves. Because much of this material has little nutritional value, they have to eat a lot of it, and spend nearly all of their time munching. In middle age they develop huge stomachs and massive intestines to hold and digest these bulky meals. In zoos, where there is usually plenty of food close at hand, they grow fatter, lazier and heavier than in the wild.

Chimpanzees and orang-utans feed mainly on fruit, but chimps also eat insects and other kinds of animal foods, for which they have to hunt. More active than orangs and gorillas, both in the wild and in zoos, chimps stay slimmer well into middle age.

ORANG-UTANS, CHIMPANZEES and gorillas are all larger and more heavily built than monkeys or gibbons. Big orangs and chimpanzees can stretch up as tall as small humans, and grow much heavier. Gorillas grow as tall as fully grown humans, and are very heavy, muscular animals.

Orang-utans live only in the forests of southeastern Asia. They stay mainly in the trees, although they are much less agile than gibbons. Orang-utans nearly always have long, reddish-brown hair and are thus very different in appearance from the other apes.

The two chimpanzee species and the much larger gorilla live in the forests of west and central Africa. They live mainly on the ground, usually walking or scampering on all fours with their fingers folded so that their knuckles take much of the weight. Gorillas and chimps look quite similar when young, but gorillas always have black faces. Young chimps have pink faces, although they usually become brown or even black as they get older.

Chimpanzees seem to be the most intelligent of the apes - that is, mentally closest to humans and quickest in their way of thinking, solving puzzles and making and using tools. This probably reflects their modes of living. Browsing on leaves and fruit makes few demands on the intellects of orang-utans and gorillas.

Gorilla (male)

Chimpanzee (male)

Fossil apes

An 11-year-old orang-utan

Chimpanzees spend part of their time hunting, which is far more demanding, and more likely to sharpen their wits. Recent chemical studies of chimpanzee blood suggest that the chimps really are our closest animal relatives.

FOSSIL MONKEYS AND APES

Fossils of monkeys, apes and early humans are rarely found complete. When the original animals died, other animals probably ate them, and scattered their bones, leaving only fragments of bones, incomplete skulls and bits of skeletons. Palaeontologists who study these remnants may find only half a lower jaw with three or four teeth, the front or base of a skull, a fragment of pelvis or other parts of the skeleton. There are usually several, scattered over a wide area, that may be from one animal or several animals. From these, using their knowledge of modern and fossil skeletons, the scientists have to 'reconstruct', or build up, models of what the original animals looked like, and decide whether they were monkeys, apes or early humans. Sometimes this becomes guesswork, or at least a matter for different scientists to disagree over.

Orang-utan (male)

During the past few million years there have been dozens of species of ape-like animals. If they were alive today, we would call them great apes. Today we have only two species of chimpanzee and one species each of gorilla and orang-utan. What happened to all the others is uncertain. Most of them are represented only in small pieces of jaws, teeth and other bones, rarely as complete skeletons. Some kinds were widespread and survived over millions of years. Others were more local, and seem to have died out more quickly.

Proconsul This genus contains some of the earliest fossil apes. Found in East Africa, the fossils are up to 20 million years old. Some were up to chimpanzee size, with large, projecting front teeth, large canines and small grinding teeth. They probably walked on all-fours and spent at least part of their time in trees.

Australopithecus Between 5 and 3 million years ago, several members of the genus *Australopithecus* appeared with ape-like skulls but with limbs more like those of humans. Up to 1.5 m (5 ft) tall, they probably walked on two legs. Some may have made and used simple tools. One of these species eventually gave rise to the first humans.

Paranthropus This genus contains several species living between 2.5 and 1 million years ago. They were related to *Australopithecus*, but had broader faces, heavier jaws and more massive grinding teeth. They stood up to about 1.2 m (4 ft) tall and probably resembled small gorillas in appearance and way of life.

Chimpanzees Very few fossils of chimpanzees (or of gorillas or orang-utans) have been found, so we do not know how long they have existed.

Skull of Proconsul africanus

Skull of Australopithecus africanus

Skull of Paranthropus robustus

Skull of chimpanzee

GIGANTOPITHECUS

This was a group of large apes that lived from about 6 million to about 1 million years ago. We know them only from fragments of jaws and teeth, which show that they were mainly vegetarian. However, they must have been enormous – much bigger than humans, and probably bigger than even the largest living gorillas. They probably lived on the ground in open country.

GREAT APES: ORANG-UTANS

Solitary 'old men' of the Indonesian rainforests.

FACT FILE

Suborder:	Anthropoidea
Family:	Pongidae
Scientific name:	*Pongo pygmaeus*
Colour:	Reddish-brown to black
Weight:	Males 70 kg (154 lb), females 45 kg (100 lb)
Length, head and body:	Males 1 m (40 in), females 80 cm (30 in)
Habitat:	Trees and shrubs in rainforest
Range:	Borneo and Sumatra

Adult female orang-utan

RELATIONSHIPS

Orang-utans are large, often tubby and ponderous great apes of southeastern Asia. They are larger and heavier than monkeys, more spider-like than chimpanzees, and far less bulky than gorillas. Like their gibbon cousins and neighbours, they are tree-living apes, though they lack gibbons' grace and agility. Whereas gibbons seem almost to fly through the tree-tops, orang-utans swing slowly like long-armed sacks among the lower branches, pausing to hang thoughtfully from one hand and scratch with the other. The two areas in which they live, separated by wide and deep water, are populated by two subspecies:

- Bornean orang-utan, *Pongo pygmaeus pygmaeus*
- Sumatran orang-utan, *Pongo pygmaeus abelii*

THE DENSE GREEN FORESTS of Indonesia are the home of several kinds of monkeys and gibbons, and one kind of great ape – the orang-utan. The name means 'old man of the forest' – and mature adults of both sexes have the worn, stooped appearance of old men, with long, untidy hair, wrinkled skin and thin straggling beards.

On the ground, orangs walk clumsily on all fours, taking part of the weight on their short legs, and part on the longer arms. However, they spend as much time as possible in the trees, where they probably feel safer and more at home. Young ones climb and swing with skill and daring, grasping the branches with slender hands and finger-like toes. Older ones, more heavy and solidly built, move slowly and deliberately, swinging with great care as though afraid of falling.

Orang-utans feed mainly on fruit, including figs, mangoes, durians and plantains, of which different kinds ripen at different times of the year. If fruit is scarce, they eat insects, leaves, shoots and roots. Where local people grow crops and vegetables, orangs sometimes make themselves unpopular by stealing, though normally they stay well away from farms and plantations. Occasionally they catch and eat lizards or birds.

Sumatran subspecies

Bornean subspecies

Broad flanges on the faces of adult males make them look bigger and fiercer when they challenge other males

Where they live

Young captive orang

Adult male

FAMILY LIFE

Male orang-utans are solitary animals who seem to prefer their own company to any other. Their loud roaring calls, amplified in large, pendulous throat pouches, echo through the forests, announcing their presence in a feeding range they consider their own, and warning others to keep away. Ranges often overlap, so several males may find themselves feeding together

Mother and baby orang

when a particular tree bears its fruit. They seldom quarrel. If there is plenty for all, eating is more profitable than fighting. However, noisy quarrels and fights break out from time to time, and most old males bear bites, deep scratches and other battle scars.

Females, too, keep their own company, but usually have a baby or one or two juveniles up to six or seven years old in attendance. When ready for mating, a female responds positively to the call of a male, approaching and feeding close to him. After mating several times, she wanders away, still leading her young from previous matings. Gestation takes about 38 weeks. The babies grow slowly, taking seven or more years to reach complete independence.

Orang-utans once lived as far north as northern China, and as far west as India. As humans spread, orangs became easy prey. Many were hunted for food, and more disappeared as the forests were cleared for agriculture. Today we find them only on the islands of Sumatra and Borneo, living in the densest parts of the rainforest. Even there they are very much at risk, for their forests are being felled for timber, and without the forest, orangs cannot survive.

For the past 40 years Indonesia and other heavily forested countries have tried to improve the wealth and living conditions of their people by exploiting these forests, cutting down the trees and exporting the timber. In some parts of Indonesia this has resulted in severe losses of the primary (original) forest, which took many years to mature and will take many more years to recover. When the forest is cut, orang-utans and monkeys lose their feeding territories. To find new ones they have to invade the territories of others, then perhaps move again a few weeks later as the cutting continues. Large areas of forest are also burned to make way for farming. The smoke from the fires can cause serious damage to the environment hundreds of kilometres away.

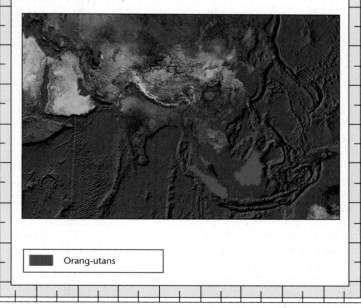

█ Orang-utans

SCHOOL FOR ORANG-UTANS

Baby orang-utans are popular as pets in many parts of Indonesia. Though buying and selling them is illegal, hunters have for many years hunted mothers with babies, shooting the mothers and selling the babies into captivity. While still young, the orphans make friendly, responsive pets. As they grow older and stronger, they become bored, cross and destructive, more so if they are chained or confined to cages. Then their owners want to get rid of them. They cannot be released into the wild, because they have never learnt how to forage for food, avoid predators or respond to other orangs.

Conservation groups in Borneo and Sumatra have been organized to rescue young orangs from captivity, bring them together in 'schools' in the forest, and gradually get them used to foraging for themselves. After a few days in cages, they are released to wander, but lured back to the safety of the 'school' by an evening feed. After a few weeks of learning, some set off on their own into the wild, others are taken to remote parts of the forest and released. Schooling does not guarantee their survival, but increases their chances of making a normal life for themselves.

GREAT APES: CHIMPANZEES

Our nearest animal relatives, chimpanzees live in central and west Africa.

FACT FILE

Suborder:	Anthropoidea
Family:	Pongidae
Scientific name:	*Pan troglodytes*
Colour:	Thin dark brown to black fur, grey or pink skin
Weight:	40 kg (88 lb)
Length, head and body:	85 cm (33 in)
Habitat:	Tropical rainforest and grassland
Range:	West, central and eastern Africa

RELATIONSHIPS

Scientists used to think there was one kind of chimpanzee, living in the dense forests that stretch across the middle of Africa. Then a few years ago came reports of a slightly smaller race or subspecies in a wet and tropical stretch of forest in east-central Congo DR, between the Congo and Lualaba rivers. Eventually scientists decided that this was a separate species, which they called the pygmy chimpanzee, and the local Africans call 'bonobo' (see page 12 for Fact File). Its scientific name is *Pan paniscus*, showing that it is closely related to the common chimpanzee. Although they belong to a different family, chimpanzees are our nearest living relatives.

Both kinds of chimpanzees have thin, shiny dark brown or black fur. Young ones have a prominent white patch on the lower back, which they lose as they grow older. Their faces are bare, showing different expressions like human smiles and frowns. Common chimpanzee males grow slightly larger and heavier than females. Pygmy chimpanzee males and females are similar, and the largest is only as big as a well-grown female common chimpanzee. The most striking difference is in the faces. As they grow older, common chimpanzees develop a longer jaw and heavier brow ridges. Pygmy chimpanzees keep a round, young-looking face throughout life.

YOU SELDOM SEE ONE CHIMPANZEE of either species on its own. Usually they live together in small bands, perhaps two or three mothers with young, accompanying one old male and two or three younger ones. Chimpanzees in a band behave as a family. The old male is the father figure, dominating the others, threatening and leading attacks on other bands that move too close. He takes the lead in moving from one area to another, in a constant search for ripe fruits and new shoots. Younger males give way to the older ones, learning from them and taking over leadership as they mature.

Within the families they keep close to each other, grooming each other's fur, removing twigs and parasites. Older ones play with the young, sometimes threatening, sometimes smacking or biting

gently if they misbehave. Young chimpanzees are light enough to climb readily and swing from tree branches. Older ones become too heavy, and tend to stay on the ground, climbing only to find fruit and to make a leafy nest for sleeping at night.

Using a stick to dig out termites

Two adult chimps with their young

Where they live

Where food is plentiful in an area, several bands come together, forming groups of up to 100 or more. When the food becomes scarce, the bands quarrel among themselves and go their separate ways to search for more. While much of their food lies in the forests, chimpanzees sometimes come into conflict with farmers, whose plantations and farms bear rich crops of figs, bananas and other fruit in season.

Family group of chimps sitting in a tree

A helping hand from mother

FAMILY LIFE

Chimpanzees are mainly vegetarian. Fruit forms the major part of their diet, but they also eat leaves, shoots, flowers and roots dug from the soft earth. In the rainforest, different species of trees flower and produce their fruits at different times of the year, so the bands are travelling constantly. Younger males learn from the older ones where food is to be found in different seasons. Chimpanzees also search bark and fallen logs for insects, and break into nests of termites and bees, using sticks and stones as tools. They take birds' eggs and chicks, and small mammals, including monkeys.

Chimps breed throughout the year. When a female is ready to mate, she gives off a scent that may attract other males to the band. The band leader is the one most likely to mate with her, but younger males may be successful too. She bears a single baby about eight months later. The baby holds on to the mother's fur, at first drinking milk from her breasts. Then, clinging to her shoulder, it learns to share the different kinds of food that she eats herself. Mothers and young stay together for two or three years, sometimes longer.

Common chimpanzees live in the dense rainforests of tropical Africa, from Senegal in the west through Nigeria, Cameroon, Gabon and Congo DR to Uganda and Tanzania in the east. Formerly numerous, they are now becoming much rarer because of hunting and local destruction of the forest for timber and agriculture. Pygmy chimpanzees have a more restricted range in the equatorial forests of eastern Congo DR. No one knows how many there are, but we do know that they are at risk as human populations continue to expand (see page 42).

■	Common chimpanzees
□	Pygmy chimpanzees

HOW HUMAN?

Scientists tell us that chimpanzees differ from us only slightly – less than any other ape – in genetic make-up. It is not surprising, therefore, that chimpanzees can be trained to sit on chairs for a zoo tea party, pour tea from a teapot and throw buns around, making them act more or less like ill-behaved children. For television commercials they can be trained to wear suits, dresses and bonnets. With human voices added, they can be made to look human enough to be living next door.

However, this training hides some important features that make chimpanzees very different from humans. Their limbs, for example, are proportionately longer than ours. They walk on all fours as much as on two legs, and their big toes, like their thumbs, can be used for gripping. Though more clumsy than we are at walking and running, they are stronger for their weight, and young ones are better at climbing and moving through trees. They are almost completely covered with body hair, except for their faces, which are mobile

and expressive like our own.

One important similarity is their ability to make and use tools. They can make a digging stick, for example, by stripping leaves off a branch, and they can join sticks together to use as a lever. To threaten they can wave clubs or bang them on the ground. They can throw branches or stones, though not very accurately, at enemies or predators.

An important difference is their use of sound. They have many different calls, from screams to muttering, which express their feelings or needs. But they have never developed use of words to express ideas. For important similarities and differences in brain structure, and other aspects of behaviour, see pages 40-41.

FACT FILE

Suborder:	Anthropoidea
Family:	Pongidae
Scientific name:	*Gorilla gorilla*
Colour:	Dark brown to blue-black
Weight:	Males 160 kg (350 lb), females 90 kg (200 lb)
Height:	Males 1.7 m (5 ft 7 in), females 1.5 m (4 ft 11 in)
Habitat:	Tropical lowland and mountain forest
Range:	Central Africa

Lowland gorilla baby 2 months old

RELATIONSHIPS

There are three quite separate populations of gorillas, generally similar in appearance but different enough in detail to be called subspecies:

- Western lowland gorilla, *Gorilla gorilla gorilla*
- Eastern lowland gorilla, *Gorilla gorilla graueri*
- Mountain gorilla *Gorilla gorilla beringei.*

Eastern gorillas tend to be darker than western, with heavier jaws and brow ridges. Mountain gorillas have shorter arms and longer fur. Formerly these populations must have intermingled, but they are now geographically isolated, with little or no contact between them in the wild.

LIFE OF GORILLAS

Gorillas share with orang-utans the longest gestation periods of all the big apes. Their babies are born some 36 or 37 weeks after a successful mating – about two weeks shorter than in humans. Gorilla babies feed on their mothers' milk for at least three years, then the young take a further nine or ten years to reach adult size and sexual maturity. They may live a further 25-30 years.

GREAT APES: GORILLAS

The largest living apes, found in mountain and lowland forests of Africa.

GORILLAS MOVE THROUGH the undergrowth in bands, usually of up to a dozen, but sometimes as many as 30. You always know when they are about. Largest of the apes, much larger than most other animals that share their forests, they have little to fear and nothing to hide. When a band is near, you hear them pushing through the undergrowth, grunting quietly to each other, occasionally barking or beating their chests with a hollow sound. If one sees you, it roars to let others know there is an intruder.

The dominant male of the party, huge and silver-backed, and some of the younger males may threaten with more chest-beating and roaring. They may charge, which usually means that you have approached too suddenly, and startled them. However, gorillas are peace-loving animals, more likely to disappear quietly into the forest than to waste energy in chasing strangers.

Other signs of their presence are crudely built nests of leaves and branches, on the ground or in low bushes, where they have slept overnight, and patches of vegetation, some eaten, the rest trampled and rolled over. Wherever they go, gorillas leave a persistent musky scent, which may warn other bands of their presence.

FAMILY LIFE

Wandering in bands through the forest, gorillas feed almost entirely on leaves, shoots and roots, and occasionally on fruit, which they pluck and manipulate with their hands. The front teeth are sharp-edged for biting, the back teeth broad and flattened for grinding vegetation. Because leaves and shoots have little nourishment and are hard to digest, gorillas have to eat huge amounts to obtain the energy they need. This may be one reason for their large stomachs.

Gorillas breed throughout the year. A female mates with one or several males within the group, and gives birth to a single baby some 36 or 37 weeks later. Weighing about 2.3 kg (5 lb) at birth, the baby holds tight to the mother's fur, travelling wherever she goes, and growing quickly on her milk. After three to four months a baby can roll and play with others of the band, and be tended and guarded by other mothers as well as its own.

Young gorilla swinging; older ones grow too fat and heavy

Mountain gorilla family group

Where they live

Western lowland gorillas live in the rainforests of Cameroon, Gabon, Congo Republic and Nigeria, west of the River Congo, on the coastal plains and mountains up to about 1,800 m (6,000 ft). Eastern lowland gorillas live in forests of eastern Congo DR, between the River Lualaba and the Great Rift Valley, at heights of up to about 2,400 m (8,000 ft). Mountain gorillas live in highland forests that grow on a range of volcanic peaks north and west of Lake Kivu, on the borderland of Congo DR, Uganda and Rwanda. This is a cloudy, damp and often cold environment, at heights of 2,700-3,700 m (9,000-12,000 ft). Their slightly longer and denser fur may help them to keep warm on chilly mornings.

- Western lowland gorilla
- Eastern lowland gorilla
- Mountain gorilla

Afternoon siesta up a tree

WHERE HAVE THEY GONE?

Within the equatorial forest, gorillas were almost certainly more plentiful and widespread in the past. The explorers who first identified them were horrified. They seemed like huge, fierce hairy people, much larger and more threatening than other humans, and much to be feared. Though gorillas are in fact gentle animals, and very unlikely to attack humans, many were shot on sight.

We do not know how many gorillas are left in the world today because they are difficult to count. Recent estimates suggest about 100,000 in the western lowlands, between 5,000 and 10,000 in the eastern lowlands, and perhaps fewer than 600 in the mountains. Populations are declining because huge areas of forest have been, and continue to be, cut down for timber or cleared for farming. Destroying the gorillas' home is the surest way to destroy gorillas (see pages 42-43), but recent wars have also caused destruction – many gorillas have been killed by soldiers for food.

Lowland gorilla

THE HUMAN FAMILY

Ground-living primates that have reached the top of the tree.

FACT FILE	
MODERN HUMAN	
Suborder:	Anthropoidea
Family:	Hominidae
Scientific name:	*Homo sapiens*
Colour:	Variable, pink to black; head and (male) face hairy, sparse body hair, usually clothed
Weight:	Varies; males heavier, on average, than females
Height:	Varies; males taller, on average, than females
Habitat:	All habitats, tropical to polar
Range:	Worldwide

RELATIONSHIPS

Human beings belong to the family Hominidae, which also contains several extinct species. Although we differ a good deal in skin colour and hair form, all living people belong to a single species – *Homo sapiens*. This name means 'wise man'. Earlier humans, with smaller brains, belonged to different species of *Homo*.

WHAT IMPORTANT DIFFERENCES set humans apart from apes and other animals?

■ *Upright stance* Apes need support when standing upright. With a different shape of pelvis, 'S'-curved spine, and angled skull, humans stand upright normally and easily.

■ *Walking* When walking, apes support their upper body on their long arms, touching the ground with their knuckles. Humans walk upright, rolling on the feet from heel to toe, leaving hands and arms free.

■ *Diet, jaws and teeth* Apes have large teeth and jaws, both for grinding vegetable food and for fighting. Eating a mixed diet, and fighting with hands and weapons, humans get by with much smaller jaws, teeth and facial muscles.

■ *Brain size* The largest apes have brains of up to about 600 cm³ (35 in³) in volume. Early humans of similar body size had brains approaching twice that volume, and modern man has brains of 1,500-2,000 cm³ (90-120 in³). Much of the extra brain gives humans more efficient memories and ways of thinking.

■ *Language* Apes express simple ideas with calls and grunts. They can be trained to recognize human words, but cannot speak them and have no equivalent words of their own. We think and express thoughts in strings of words, called language, and can record them in different ways to pass from one generation to the next.

Where they lived

- *Making and using tools* Apes use stones or twigs as tools, and may shorten twigs to make them more efficient for particular purposes. Humans make and use tools all the time, from spades to bulldozers, from scooters to intercontinental aircraft.
- *Growing up* Young apes take 10-12 years to become adults. Human children can breed from about 12 years, but do not stop growing until they are 18-20, and may then spend several more years in education.
- *Communities* Monkeys and apes live in troops or bands that keep together by sight, hearing and touch. Language and technology enable humans to live in much bigger groups, from villages to cities of several million inhabitants.
- *Other differences* Can you think of other ways in which humans differ from other animals?

The earliest near-human fossil remains appear in Olduvai Gorge, East Africa, and are about 1.75 million years old. Though given the name *Homo habilis*, meaning 'skilful man', they are now thought to represent small, semi-upright apes, with a brain capacity of 700 cm³ (40 in³), which lived in a dry, warm climate, and hunted in grassland and along the forest edge.

The earliest remains that are generally agreed to be human have been found at several sites, including central Java, China, Africa and Europe. Though all were given separate names when discovered, they are now bundled together as *Homo erectus* ('upright man'). Dating from about 1 million to 300,000 years ago, they represent a small kind of human with a brain capacity of 900-1,000 cm³ (50-60 in³), who hunted, and used simple tools and fire.

Homo sapiens ('wise man'), our own species, appears first in fossil deposits about 250,000 years old. These too are widespread, and vary in size and proportions between sites. Skulls and other bones dating from about 40,000 years ago are virtually identical to those of modern humans. *Homo sapiens* also spread across Africa, Europe and Asia, and was the only human species to spread to North and South America, crossing the Bering Bridge (then dry land, now the Bering Strait) about 12,000 years ago.

Though originally a species of warm grassland and forest edge, humans have adapted to every climate and habitat from the hottest, wettest tropical forests to some of the driest deserts.

African bushman of today

HUMAN POPULATION GROWTH

For many thousands of years the human population remained small. While we lived in small groups, hunting and gathering our food like other primates, there were probably just a few hundred thousand of us world-wide. Then we began to grow food instead of hunting for it, live in villages instead of wandering bands, manufacture goods and trade with each other, and our population began expanding.

Now there are some six billion of us, and we have come to dominate the world.

WHERE DID HUMANS COME FROM?

Most biologists believe that all the different kinds of animals we see around us today evolved from earlier forms. Ancestors were similar to living forms, but not exactly the same. For example, if we could go back five million years, we would see elephants, deer and bears similar to, but not quite like, modern ones, as well as similar but different monkeys, apes and humans. Farther back in time we would find small creatures from which all of today's mammals, including elephants, deer, bears and primates, evolved.

The naturalist Charles Darwin gave the most popular explanation of how this process (called evolution) came about.

He saw that individuals within groups of animals varied slightly between themselves. Those that were stronger or better suited than others to their surroundings lived and produced many offspring. Others that were weaker or less suited died before they had a chance to breed, or for other reasons produced fewer offspring. So the 'useful' characteristics were passed on to new generations. But the environment was not the same everywhere, so populations in one area changed in different ways from those elsewhere. Over millions of years, plants and animals evolved into all sorts of different species.

Darwin called this process 'natural selection', and felt that it applied as much to humans as to all other animals and plants. Not everyone agrees. Some, including some biologists, believe that the differences between species are too great to have been produced in this way. Others believe that humans are so different from all other forms of life that they must have been created specially. What do you think?

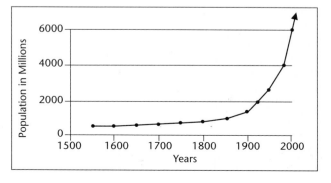

Population in Millions vs Years (1500–2000)

ENDANGERING OTHER ANIMALS

Of the countless different species of animals that have lived on earth, hundreds of thousands no longer exist. They have become extinct. Yet new species have constantly appeared to take their places.

Most of these extinctions happened before humans came on the scene. Some are happening now. There are species alive today that will disappear within the next 40-50 years, either through natural

Endangered – mountain gorilla

causes, or because humans are helping to destroy them.

When our ancestors first appeared on earth, and for a long time after, they were no more important than dozens of other kinds of medium-to-large mammals that lived at the same time. They hunted the plains and gathered food, as some monkeys and apes do today, breeding at about the same rate, living and dying much as they do.

Then gradually their ways of life changed. Perhaps their big brains and intelligence made them too successful as hunters. Certainly over tens of thousands of years they wiped out whole populations of other mammals across Asia and Europe.

Our ancestors developed tools and skills for clearing the forests, tilling the land, raising crops and domesticating animals. They dug deep for fuel and valuable minerals, and learnt to deal with injury and illness, to avoid starvation and to destroy predators. More of their babies survived and lived longer.

The result was an enormous increase in human population, from tens of thousands to millions, and then to billions. Human population continues to increase, every day demanding more and more land and resources, and edging other animals out of their homes.

MONKEYS AND APES AT RISK

Species fighting for survival.

PEOPLE CAN DESTROY populations of monkeys and apes in many ways, sometimes wilfully, sometimes accidentally.

- *Hunting for food* Villagers in many forested areas catch and kill monkeys for food. Where monkeys are plentiful, where there is plenty of forest for them to hide in, and where the villagers have other sources of food, this is not very important.
- *Hunting for pets* This can be more damaging, particularly to populations of such attractive species as marmosets and tamarins, which may already be at risk.
- *Hunting for sale to suppliers and traders* This can be very damaging. The demand may be great and, because so many die in transit, more monkeys and apes are taken than are actually needed.
- *Forest clearance* Every patch of forest cleared displaces native animals. If many areas are cut, surviving animals have fewer places for refuge. Forest clearance, which may also lead to disastrous out-of-control fires, is the main reason why so many populations of monkeys and apes are currently at risk.

Thus the most serious causes of danger are forest clearance and trading. The best ways to protect the monkeys and apes are: (1) To discover as exactly as possible their numbers and needs. (2) To prohibit all trading except under licence, and to issue licences only for species or populations known to be plentiful. (3) To ensure that logging, too, is allowed only under licence, and that large blocks of forest remain as reserves for the native animals.

Lion tamarin

Mountain gorilla

MONKEYS AND APES AT RISK

The International Union for the Conservation of Nature (IUCN), a conservation organization with headquarters in Switzerland, estimates that almost half the living species of monkeys and apes are endangered in one way or another. Here are just a few of them:

1. Lion tamarin, *Leontopithecus rosalia.* These beautiful little animals live in small remnants of forest in the hills north of Rio de Janeiro, southeastern Brazil. They are pretty enough to be much in demand as pets, and forest clearance, due to pressures of human population, has left them with very little living space. There may be only a few dozen remaining in the wild.

Lion-tailed macaque

2. Lion-tailed macaque, *Macaca silenus.* This shaggy black macaque, with a strikingly handsome grey mane and beard, lives in dense forests of the Western Ghats, a mountain range in southwest India. Named for the tuft of fur on its long tail, it is seldom seen these days, and may have been hunted almost to destruction.

3. Golden snub-nosed monkey, *Rhinopithecus roxellana.* Snub-nosed monkeys form one of the branches of the colobus monkey group (pages 26-27), distinguished by thick lips and curiously upturned nostrils. They live in mountain forests of eastern China and Vietnam. This species, the golden snub-nose, has thick brown fur laced with gold, yellow-gold feet and bright blue eye-rings. Much in demand as pets, they are becoming extremely rare in the wild.

4. Yellow-tailed woolly monkey, *Lagothrix flavicauda.* This is a big New World monkey of the cebid family (pages 18-19) that lives in damp, tropical forests of the Peruvian Andes. The name comes from a yellow stripe on the long, prehensile tail. The fur, reddish brown, is dense and velvety, and much valued by local people to decorate clothing.

5. Silvery gibbon, *Hylobates moloch.* Gibbons (pages 30-31) live almost entirely in trees. They get to know their way around their own patch of forest, and are totally lost when the chain-saws move in. This is a species whose forests on the island of Java are gradually being cut down for their valuable timber. There are probably only a few hundred of them left.

6. Sumatran orang-utan, *Pongo pygmaeus abelii.* The forest homes of these great apes are being systematically destroyed for timber and agriculture, but they are also popular as household pets – at least until they grow big enough to become a nuisance. So their numbers are declining steadily – there is an estimated 5,000-7,000 of them left.

7. Mountain gorilla, *Gorilla gorilla beringei.* The damp, overgrown forested slopes of central Africa have long been the home of these huge, gentle animals. They are shy and need plenty of space. Few remain, as gradually their forests are being taken over for agriculture.

Golden snub-nosed monkey

HOW CAN WE HELP?

- Join a national or international conservation group dedicated to protecting and conserving wildlife, especially monkeys and apes. There are several addresses on page 45.
- Help the group to raise money for research on monkeys and apes, and to support schemes for their protection.
- Learn all you can about monkeys and apes. Read about them, watch TV programmes, videos and films, and tell all your friends about them. Get as many people as you can to support their protection and conservation.
- Visit parks and reserves where monkeys and apes live. Ask the park managers, rangers or guides what species are present and how they are faring.
- Visit zoos to see how well their monkeys and apes are kept, and talk to the keepers and managers about them. Are they lively and well fed? Have they plenty of room? Are they breeding? If you feel they are badly looked-after, complain first to the manager, then to the authority that licenses the zoo and allows it to stay open.
- Remember that, where monkeys and apes live close to people, the people may be very poor. They will be tempted to kill animals that destroy their crops, or trade them in for money. Support organizations that help people, monkeys and apes to live alongside each other.
- If you live in a country that has wild monkeys and apes, encourage your national and local governments and your local community to support wildlife of all kinds, including their monkeys and apes.
- Visit national parks and reserves where monkeys and apes live, and encourage others to do the same.

Sumatran orang-utan

GLOSSARY

Can you identify the species pictured?
(answers below)

adaptation	Change in a plant or animal that increases its chances of survival
aggression	Readiness to attack
ancestors	Parents, grandparents and earlier generations
Bering Bridge	Dry land between northern Asia and North America, which existed when sea level was lower
brachiation	Swinging through the trees using the arms
canine teeth	Usually the longest, sharpest teeth, at the front corner of each jaw
canopy	Tree-tops
carnivore	Animal that feeds mainly on the flesh of other animals
conservation	Saving and protecting species, usually by protecting the places where they live
density	Number (of animals or plants) in a particular area
digestive system	Parts of an animal in which food is broken down and absorbed (mouth, throat, stomach, intestines and so on)
dominant	Most important, able to control others
equatorial	Living in the hot region around the equator
evolution	The process by which plants and animals slowly change from generation to generation, gradually giving rise to new species that are adapted to different habitats and different ways of life
extinction	The dying out of a plant or animal species, either from a particular area or from the whole world
forage	To search for food
fossil	Remnant of ancient plant or animal preserved in stone
fossil record	A sequence of fossils of different ages showing how an animal group, such as the apes, has evolved over a period of time
genus	Group of closely related animals or plants (plural, 'genera')
gestation period	Length of time it takes for baby animals to grow inside their mother
habitat	Place where a plant or animal lives
herbivore	Animal that feeds mainly on vegetation (plant life)
litter	Group of young animals that are born and raised together
mammal	Any kind of warm-blooded animal in which the female suckles her young with milk from her own body. Most mammals have hair or fur. All the primates are mammals, and so are bears and horses
mane	Long hair on the neck and shoulders
mangrove	Any of a number of small trees and shrubs with tangled roots that habitually grow in the mud around tropical coasts and estuaries
molar teeth	Teeth at the back of the mouth, used for grinding food

From top: lemur, douroucouli, colobus, orang-utan

monitoring	Watching carefully to see what progress is being made
New World	North and South America (see Old World)
nocturnal	Active by night
Old World	Europe and Asia (see New World)
omnivorous	Eating both animal and vegetable foods
palaeontologist	Scientist who studies fossils
poachers	Illegal hunters
population	Part of a species living in a particular area, sometimes but not always separated geographically from other populations of the same species
predator	Animal that hunts, kills and eats other animals
pregnant	Carrying a developing baby or babies inside the body
prehensile tail	A tail the tip of which can curl around and grasp a branch
prosimians	Monkey-like animals such as lemurs and lorises
rainforest	Forest that grows in the wettest parts of the world, especially in the hot areas around the equator where it rains nearly every day
rodents	Mammals with sharp, chisel-like front teeth, such as mice, rats and squirrels
savanna	Grassland with scattered trees and shrubs
scavenge	Eat rubbish or old food, including dead animals, that has been lying around for some time
species	A particular kind of plant or animal

Useful addresses

International Primate Protection League,
116 Judd Street, London WC1H 9NS
(Tel: 020 7837 7227)

Monkey World, Longthorns, East Stoke,
Wareham, Dorset DH20 6HH
(Tel: 01929 462537)

Durrell Wildlife Conservation Trust, Trinity,
Jersey, Channel Islands JE3 5BP
(Tel: 01534 860000)

Orangutan Foundation, 7 Kent Terrace,
London NW1 4RP (Tel: 020 7724 2912)

WWF (UK), Panda House, Weyside Park,
Cattershall Lane, Godalming,
Surrey GU7 1XR
(Tel: 01483 426 444; Fax: 01483 426 409)

WWF (Australia), Level 5, 725 George St,
Sydney, NSW 2000

WWF (South Africa), 116 Dorp Street,
Stellenbosch 7600

From top: Barbary macaque, red uakari, tarsier, pileated gibbon

INDEX